Ode to Minoa

by
Theresa C. Dintino

ISBN 1-56315-143-X

Paperback Fiction
© Copyright 1999 Theresa C. Dintino
All rights reserved
First Printing—1999
Library of Congress #98-88534

Request for information should be addressed to:

SterlingHouse Publisher, Inc.
The Sterling Building
440 Friday Road
Pittsburgh, PA 15209
www.SterlingHousePublisher.com

Cover design: Steve Czarnecki - SterlingHouse, Inc.
Typesetting: Drawing Board Studios

Printed in Canada

To Yoni,
Who believed

Acknowledgments

I must pause here to acknowledge and express my gratitude to those whose works have inspired my own and which I have drawn upon in the writing of this book. First and foremost Marija Gimbutas whose work, so thorough, heartfelt and full of integrity, allowed me to open to the Goddess. Mary Daly's courage and creative genius who inspired me to be daring. Riane Eisler's, *The Chalice and the Blade*, which encouraged me to imagine. Carolyn Heilbrun's eloquent words which started a yearning within me to write a story about a woman which did not end with death or marriage. Nancy Blair's, *Amulets of the Goddess*, which helped guide me along the way, Ted Andrew's wonderful book on animal magic and power symbols, *Animal-Speak*. Rodney Castleden's detailed and well rounded research on Minoan Crete and Her people. The works of Monica Sjöö and Barbara Mor, Vicki Noble, Adrienne Rich and many many more.

To my sister, Maria, who encouraged me always as well as generously lent me her library card. Your soulful and steadfast support serve as a foundation from which I draw on.

To the Southwest Regional Department of Libraries in Dummerston, Vermont, who found me any book I requested with a smile, I send a hearty thanks.

Part I

 **PROLOGUE**

Like any child, I believed I was born in the most wonderful place in the world. What I did not know, until I was older, was that for me it was true. Minoa and her people would be remembered with fondness for millennia.

I was born at Crete, a place of land surrounded by the bright blues and pale greens of water. A place of butterflies and dolphins and a night sky where even the stars changed colors.

In the early morning of the autumnal equinox, in the annum 1600 B.C.E., my mother slowly released me out of herself. An owl sat on one of the low branches of the fig tree outside the Cave of the Life-giving Woman. A great gray owl; waiting.

After the priestesses had bathed me in the waters of the stream which makes itself into a pool within the cave, my mother, Sheena, brought me to the owl.

She shifted her weight between her two feet several times before focusing her wide yellow eyes upon me. "Who? Who? Whooo?" she asked.

Sheena stood hypnotized, the owl's pensive stare upon her now.

"Aureillia," she finally said, naming me.

The owl spread her wings, their span so wide they seemed to fill the entire opening of the cave. She flew her slow, silent flight away from us, into the mists of the early morning air.

 CHAPTER 1

From the time we were very young, Danelle would sit for long periods of time drawing in the sand. He would create intricate, detailed pictures, then, with one quick movement of his hand, brush them out. I would beg him to draw them on clay or birch bark and give them to me to keep. He would merely click his tongue and shoo me away with his hand.

We lived in Knossos, the largest community on Crete.

Knossos sat on the north central side of the island and had a large, busy port. As a child, this port with its long docks of trade was one of my favorite places. Often in my wanderings I would end up there, listening to different languages, observing boat people from other lands, watching supplies of olive oil, wine, and large logs of cypress trees being loaded onto the ships.

Many mornings were spent with friends walking on beach sands still so damp from the presence of sea that our small feet would sink deep. With long sticks we would poke at clumps of seaweed and watch the crabs run back toward the waters. We would gather shells, starfish, shiny deposits of mineral serpentine and the perfect, full bodies of sea cucumbers. When we had a good supply it was I they would send to the port to do dealings with the boat people.

I can still remember the feel of the hot sand passing between my feet and sandals as I skipped toward the port, the pouch of sea treasures bouncing at my hip.

We were not the only children who did this. Many of the sea people made sure to have with them plenty of small polished stones. I would trade for obsidian and jade, lapis and amethyst, small pieces of bronze and copper. When I returned, we would spread my acquisitions out in the white sand, arguing and bartering over who would get what.

Once, I had found a particularly large sand dollar. It had a star design on its top and, when shaken, made a gentle rattling sound. I knew when I found it what I would trade it for. There was one woman from Anatolia who often had pink stones. I had wished for some time for a pink stone. When I arrived at the docks with my sand dollar, I immediately approached her.

After she had inspected my offering she held out a large piece of unpolished pink stone.

"It is quite large," I said, "but it is not polished."

"Yes, but with a little bit of work, it may become something," she said. "I, however, do not possess such talents."

"Nor do I," I said, having already decided I did not wish to give up my sand dollar for such a thing.

"Perhaps," she said, taking my hand and pressing the stone firmly within it, "perhaps you know someone who does."

"Please," I said, but she was speaking to someone else. I opened my hand and was surprised to see the sand dollar sitting within it still, beside the stone. I looked at her.

"Go," she said, swinging her hand at me. "Off with you."

"Thank you," I said, bowing slightly toward her.

She nodded her head.

The docks of trade flowed into a central receiving area covered with a peaked roof similar in design to the ones of the Center building beyond the hill above it. Stone walkways led away from the port up toward the Center and into Knossos herself. I followed a stone pathway until it turned into dirt, where I began to meander along the edges slowly, watching for crickets to jump out of the long grass.

I was crouched down, about to catch one when Danelle startled me. "What is it that you acquired today?" he asked.

"Thanks to you, that cricket has gotten away," I said, standing up.

"I am sorry," he said. "Better for the cricket, I suppose."

"I suppose," I said, though I did not agree. I thought crickets were quite lucky to be caught by me. "Well, what have you managed to get at the docks today?"

His question made me remember the heavy pouch dangling at my hip. "It was rather odd," I said, lifting the pouch and unraveling its tie. "A woman from Anatolia gave this to me." I held the stone up for him to see. Here in the light I saw its beauty. Still, it was very rough and impure.

"Look at that," Danelle said, leaning in toward it with his hands behind his hips. "She gave it to you?"

"She thought it could become something," I said, shrugging.

"Most definitely it may become something," he said.

"I can already see what."

"You can?"

"May I touch it?" he asked.

"You may have it," I said. "I do not care for it. I told her that, but then she didn't even take my sand dollar."

"I couldn't possibly," he said.

"Yes, you must," I said. "I am offering it to you."

"I would be most grateful..."

"Quick," I said, pushing the stone into his hands. "Take it." I leaned down and scooped my hands around a plump cricket.

Through the long days of the heated moons, Danelle carved and cut at that stone, never letting me see what he was doing. I would hear him chipping away in his room and knew that meant for me to stay away. Eventually he took what he had created, put it in a jar with some sand and fresh water, and placed it between two rocks on the cove. Through one whole lunar cycle those stones rolled around inside that pot, back and forth, over and around. We would sit together staring at it, listening to its rhythmic rocking.

Everyone has a birth story. Danelle's went like this: within the same moon that Danelle was born, a dolphin came to shore on the secluded beach where his mother, Hypia, was staying and brought forth her own young. It was a rare event indeed. Hypia took great comfort in knowing the forces of the dolphin would influence the life of the child growing within her. This was a very good thing.

Residents of Knossos lived in blocks of rooms circling a central courtyard. Each block had its own kitchen. In our block lived six mothers and their young children. The children of my childhood were the children of my block. I shared my room with my sister, Thela. Thela was two annums older than me. I also had two yet older sisters who were already initiated and lived in a different block with other initiated women.

Danelle and Hypia lived in our block. He was her one and only child. She was an intense woman. I remember her sitting silent time in her room for long periods. She worked in the clay room in the Center, creating tall urns and pithoi upon giant, spinning wheels. Danelle and I used to steal into the Center and peek through the doorway at her as she worked—knees bent and spread around the large urn spinning between them; her large, strong hands molding the edges, keeping up with the speed of the wheel.

Hypia was very active in the development of our community— the community of Minoa. She worked on many councils, including distribution of goods and festival organization. Most important, however, was her firm commitment toward preserving the ways of Minoa.

Around us the world was changing, and had been for some time. Different people from faraway places had gradually invaded the lands surrounding us, bringing with them ways unlike ours. The people in these lands were beginning to change their ways. Hypia was one of the leaders of the group of people working to keep our ways intact. She worried over it often, always speaking about how women would suffer under these new conditions. Though I was too young to understand what she was talking about, I knew from the way she spoke and the fire in her eyes that it must be terribly important.

Sheena was deeply involved with Hypia. Her mother, Rory, had been a sailor, and had indeed seen the changes happening in many different places. Sheena and Hypia shared this common concern. Many evenings I was awakened by their passionate discussions over the hearth in the central court of our block. Other times I lay listening to them share each other in my mother's room next to mine.

I was not my mother's first, yet my having been born on the autumnal equinox with the owl as my familiar made her feel she should take special care of me in my youth. I received the attention of the first with the experience of the fourth.

I can still remember her deep, sweet smell encompassing me as I drew warm, silky liquid into myself, the juices from within her flowing into me, filling my tiny, wanting, bird mouth, the back of my throat—down and through to all the extremities of my small body—until I floated upon its white creaminess.

Sheena was one of the lead weavers in the Center. She was particularly talented in mixing together different materials for increased softness and durability. Her blankets were recognized for their wide circular designs of soft blues and dark greens. After I was too large to be held by her, those blankets provided great comfort wrapped around me on cool evenings or early mornings of dense fog.

After the stones had been rolling around in the pot on the beach for a good while, Danelle handed me something wrapped in a piece of cloth. I opened it to discover a pink, carved owl. Though small, it possessed intricate detail. Its eyes were a circle within a circle within a circle with lines drawn between and connecting them—spinning wheels—covering the entire facial area.

"For me?" I asked.

"Yes. Yes. Come," he said, taking me by the arm. I followed him into his room. Near his lamp, on the table next to his bed, sat a jumping dolphin, carved out of the same pink stone.

"Danelle," I said, kneeling down to better see it. "How did you know these were in there?"

He said nothing—only smiled and shrugged his shoulders as he sat down on the bed next to me.

"Oh, how they must miss each other," I said, placing the owl next to the dolphin. "First one stone, then rolling around together all that time in that jar."

"What a strange thought," Danelle said, his lips drooping downward as he studied them.

I took my owl to the jewel room in the Center and had them drill a hole through it, that I may wear it hanging from a rope around my neck, as a pendant. I wore it always, even swimming and sleeping, removing it only on those occasional nights when I would allow it to sleep next to Danelle's dolphin.

Danelle was ruffled at first when he saw what I had done to his creation.

"I want it with me always," I said. "I cannot bear to be without it."

"I cannot believe you drilled a hole into it!" he said, grabbing it and examining it.

"It was a gift. A person may do as they wish with a gift," I said angrily.

He looked into my eyes, which looked into his defiantly. Danelle's eyes were blue, a blue at once light and dark. I became lost inside them, sinking deeper and deeper into the contrast, into the tiny fragments of glass.

He must have seen something different in mine, however, because he would always look away first. As now, his eyes pulled away from mine. He looked down at the owl, smirked and shook his head, then let go.

# CHAPTER 2

When the stone workers in the Center saw Danelle's work, they immediately recruited him. Every other afternoon he would go there as an apprentice.

The Center building in Knossos was the largest of all the Centers on the island. By the time I was a child it had become vast in size and function, containing over nine hundred rooms as well as central plumbing.

The building was set on a small hill in the center of a fertile valley covered with cultivated fields and groves of trees. A a swift hike to the north was the sea.

Built around a central rectangular open-air courtyard, the Center sprawled herself in long corridors and wide, curving staircases three levels tall. The west wing was reserved for the temples of the Goddess, living quarters for priestesses and priests, columned ceremonial and processional halls. The east wing contained Her many workshops and storage for the goods such activities produced. The higher levels were reserved for administrative purposes.

Each annum, after the harvest was in and before the rains, the people of Knossos would celebrate the festival of the bees. All the residents would put all of their energies into creating whatever had been decided upon for that year. It is in this way that the larger building projects of the community, which required many hands and much hard labor were carried out.

By the time of my youth, Knossos already had herself two marinas—a small one for our own fishing boats and a larger one for trade—stone walkways and roadways stretching in all directions as well as aqueducts to Knossos and drainage systems from.

One year the Goddess was particularly demanding. She asked the council of elders, whose job it was to consult Her about what project they should undertake, to build a labyrinthine course beneath the Center floors.

"Let there be a place," She had said, "for the people of Minoa to come and experience me."

Because they were not sure of Her meaning, the council of elders stayed on Moon Mountain an extra night. That night they drank the broth of the poppy and waited by the fire. Still nothing came to them. A few nights later, however, they all received the same dream. In the dream they were all shown the sacred labyrinth. It took a very long time for them to pass what they had seen to the Center architects. It took an even longer time for the architects to understand how to build it. For three consecutive festivals of the bees, all the people of Knossos worked harder than they ever had before on the sacred labyrinth.

In my youth, I was not aware of what it was used for. I had heard stories of people going mad inside it from lack of space and light. I had heard of people passing through quickly—amazing others with their speed. It was always emphasized, however, whether they passed through it fast or slow, that they emerged from the labyrinth a different person than they had been before they went in.

During the festivals people had the opportunity of meeting others of the community that they did not ordinarily have much contact with. Each annum, everyone was assigned a different task. One time I worked in the central kitchen, preparing soups, cakes and breads for the meal times. Everything that we cooked had to contain honey as one of its ingredients, in honor of the bees. Another time, I was a bee dancer in the opening and closing ceremonies.

My favorite time was the annum I was assigned to help build a road. I loved going to the quarries and chipping away at the stone. My sister Thela and I chipped under the supervision of a man larger than any I had known before. He towered above us, his heavy voice booming out commands. He taught us how to cut a perfect square of stone, load it onto the wagon, and place it in a perfectly matched hole dug into the earth. Often when I walk that road, now smoothed over from years of feet and wagons passing over it, I think of how my girl hands were involved in its creation. Now, just another part of our island. One can hardly remember a time when it had not been there—a time before.

I saw less and less of Danelle. Between our lessons in the Center and his apprenticeship, his days were filled up. Luckily, we had one lesson together: sitting silent time. The teacher was Tolles, a small, thin man with short, thick, black hair and skin darkened from the sun.

He was calm and patient, with a keen ability for listening—the perfect temperament for teaching young people silent time.

We would bustle in there from the beaches, the waters, the groves, our bodies pulsing with excitement. Where it would have taken another person the entire session to calm us down, Tolles needed only to sit in the center of the circle he had us form around him and be still.

Sitting silent time was one of the most important lessons taught at the Center. It was said that if a person practiced silent time often, she gained better control over herself and her actions, as well as greater access to other realms. It was especially recommended for times of high activity.

Danelle had taken to it at once, sitting close to Tolles, absorbing every word, every stance, every gesture. He practiced frequently outside of lesson, often trying to get me to join him, but I cared not for it. I only longed to roam the island under the guidance of the sun, bathing in Her warm waters, following after butterflies.

After a time, Tolles began to come to our block to see Danelle in the evenings. They would sit by the fire, visiting, or journey together into the caves far up on the mountain peaks. Danelle never invited me to join them in their fireside chats or hiking excursions.

"What is going on between those two?" I said to Sheena one night after I had watched them walk away together. "Danelle acts like he doesn't even know me when Tolles is around."

"It means a lot to a son when he finds his father," Sheena said.

"His father?" I said, taken aback by her answer.

"Yes. Danelle is very lucky and he knows it. It does not often happen so nicely as it happened with him. To have known him already as a teacher and admired him so."

"What?" I asked, shaking my head in confusion. Sheena motioned for me to sit down. I sat myself upon a mat close to the fire. I felt intensely perturbed. Why had Danelle not told me himself?

"Aureillia, Danelle is completely enraptured by this discovery. Try to understand."

I took some deep breaths to calm myself, then grew even more agitated at the thought that it was Tolles who had taught me this practice. I took a few more breaths into that thought, and when I had succeeded in calming myself a little, I looked at Sheena.

"I'm ready to listen now," I said.

"Hypia has always known that Tolles was Danelle's father," Sheena began. "Their relationship was brief. She was so stunned by the discovery of new life moving in her waters that she went into seclusion until well after Danelle was born.

"After Danelle had been in class for a while, Tolles began to wonder about him. One day he saw Hypia talking to Danelle in one of the corridors in the Center, and then he was sure. That evening he came to see Hypia to ask if he was the father of Danelle."

I looked at Sheena. "I do not understand," I said.

"You see, Aureillia, a woman is not allowed to tell a man the identity of a child unless he comes seeking. This way, the man comes to his child out of desire and not obligation. The relationship is pure. If a man comes seeking, which he usually does, she is required to give him the most honest answer she can: 'Yes,' 'No,' or 'I don't know.' It is very difficult sometimes for a woman to determine who the father is, but she usually has a knowing."

I thought about this, about how Danelle was so like Hypia and yet also so like Tolles. I had noticed similarities between him and Tolles even before I had known this. I felt happy for Danelle, especially in knowing how much he admired Tolles. I still wished he had told me. But suddenly, it occurred to me why he had not.

"Sheena," I said, though I was hesitant to ask, "why has my father not come seeking after me?"

"Aureillia, my darling, now is the time for you to understand why you know not of these things." Sheena took my hand into hers and brushed the hair back on my head. "Your father did come seeking. The moment I emerged from the Cave of Life-giving Woman, after the owl flew away, there your father stood. 'Am I the father of Aureillia?' he asked."

Sheena's eyes had a dreaminess I had never before seen in them. I was shocked by this addition to the story I had heard so often.

"'Yes,' I said, 'you are the father of Aureillia.' He took you in his arms and nestled your tiny body near his face." She shook her head and took a deep breath.

"Aureillia," she said, looking at me, "I am sorry to have to tell you that the man who fathered you was taken back shortly after you were born."

"Oh, my," I said. I was full of so many feelings, yet most stunned by Sheena, by the person I had just seen in that memory. Where had she gone? As though hearing my thoughts, she continued.

"It was a very difficult loss for me. We were very good friends. His name was Marcelles. What a person! Full of passion and the burning fires of achievement. He was one of the main architects in the temple of the Bee Goddess. It was his mind that thought up so many of the things you see around you, the things that make Knossos what it is. He imagined things—grand things—then he put all his energy into making them real. He was very serious, like you."

"Serious?" I had never thought of myself in that way.

"Yes. He spent a lot of time thinking, searching."

She had on a maroon dress which showed the dark hues of her skin, the deep sheen of her hair. I suddenly felt like I knew nothing about her, and I wanted to know. I wanted to know this part of her.

"He got so inflamed about his own ideas. Every time I saw him he would greet me with, 'You'll never guess what I thought of to-day.' And he was right. I never could," she said, laughing to herself. "His exuberance carried people in a wave of excitement through the most difficult undertakings during the festival of the bees. Oh, Marcelles—I miss him still."

"What happened to him, Sheena? Why is he no longer with us?"

She straightened the cloth of her dress upon her lap, then crossed her arms upon it. "At the time it was the most horrible thing," she said. "I was so very angry. He was taken back in an accident during the festival of the bees. It was the annum we were building the marina, the one for trade. He had been so excited about it, spending the whole annum thinking about it and planning. "He envisioned it as a virtual welcome to Minoa herself. He said for some people it would be their first impression of Knossos, of Minoa, and so it should show her.

"That is why the marina is so impressive and so mirrors the Center in design and structure. The marina of trade was Marcelles' greatest triumph."

She was looking into the fire now; my hand was in hers but she was not with me. "It was toward the end of the festival. The facade was completed. He was very satisfied with the results. It was time to lay down the docks. Large, heavy chunks of limestone were being hauled down the hill and led out into the water to be put down as a support. Marcelles was extremely tired. He had been working so hard. I kept telling him to calm himself," she said, lifting my hand within hers up into the air, "to rest. But he would not. He was driven.

"He was leading the block of limestone through the water to try to position it on top of the other blocks. It was at the deep end of the docks. It was exhausting work. He got pinned underneath the block somehow, when they set it on top of the other one. By the time they were able to lift it off him, he was gone.

"Everyone was so saddened and upset. They ordered all work stopped on the marina for three whole days, until Marcelles was returned properly. I argued against this, saying Marcelles would never have wanted us to stop, but to press on. But the people did not feel inclined to do this and they were right. Rest was needed."

I thought of all the time I had spent down at the port, never once knowing that the man who had fathered me had been taken back there. I thought about how much I liked the marina and how I loved lingering at the docks, and I wondered about that.

"I'm so sorry that you should not know him, Aureillia. Thela, she's more like me, but not you. You are very much like Marcelles. It has always been hard for me to keep up with you, but for Marcelles it would not have been difficult."

"Thela?" I said.

"Yes. He fathered her as well. He passed many hours with Thela, but she does not remember. She was only a baby."

For days after that, I struggled for a memory of him. I tried to remember myself as a tiny baby in Sheena's arms and to see if he was anywhere in these memories, his voice as he spoke to her, or even a memory of him holding me—but I was unable to evoke any. Thela had nothing to offer me either, remembering nothing of the man.

I continuously bothered Sheena with question after question, which she answered graciously and patiently. Finally, one day she said to me, "Come. We will honor him at the mountain sanctuary. You shall feel better. Go tomorrow to the temple of the Butterfly and request two of the copper labrys."

# CHAPTER 3

The temple of the Butterfly was on the second level of the Center. In the hallway directly outside it, large windows allowed air to circulate in the temple itself. The doors were wide open and welcoming, but I walked through them timidly. I had never entered this temple before.

The inside was partitioned off with many different colored walls of silk. Purple, red, pink, and green sheets of sleek, fine fabric hung down from the ceiling, lightly brushing the temple floor. The wind from the open windows in the hallway blew in, moving them with a gentle, almost musical rustling sound across the floor.

In the entryway sat a priestess at a table covered with tools. Her head was down as she concentrated on carving into one of the copper blades of a double axe—a labrys. I stood above her for a time, watching her form a meticulous winged spiral.

"I have come to request two of the copper labrys," I said finally.

"For what do you require them?" she asked, not looking up.

"I am going to the mountain sanctuary," I said, "to remember someone."

"Someone you knew?"

"I did not know him, but it is he who fathered me." The priestess stopped her work and looked up at me.

She was older than I had expected her to be. Her face showed many years and, while her hair was dark in the back, in the front it was a most bright white. Her eyes were deep black with the slightest yellow edging.

"This is very difficult," she said, "to only hear tell of someone important to you."

"Yes," I said, backing away from her. Her eyes frightened me a bit. "That is true. That is how I feel."

"For this you need gold, not copper," she said, standing up. "Why do you request two?"

"My mother will come with me."

"Your mother will have copper," she said. She motioned toward a bench set against the wall behind me. "Sit. I will soon return."

I watched her walk away from me down a long corridor of silk. Again, from behind, she appeared to be a young woman. She had a light skip in her walk and her back was straight and supple. I went and sat myself down on the bench. I listened to the mystic rustling of the curtains.

When she returned, she carried a labrys in each hand, the blades turned upward. One was a small copper one, similar to the one she had been carving. The other was a large gold one. I was astounded by its size and could not believe it was for me. It was as long as a tall flower. The double blades unfolded in wide swinging arcs away from its center. Their curving edges were polished smooth. On each blade was engraved a butterfly and the circling spirals of life.

"This is the labrys of recollection," she said, sitting beside me, showing it to me. "Sometimes it is possible to contact people after they have left us. If your father's spirit is accessible and you perform the ritual of the golden labrys, you may hear from him in some way."

Her white hair was cut around her face in the front, bordering her forehead and angling down around the sides. Through her speaking and facial movements, she was able to change her appearance in an uncanny fashion; looking once energetic, once worn out, once stern, once joyful.

"Realize, of course, that there are many different ways that beings from differing planes contact us, and keep yourself open. There is also the possibility that nothing will happen. If this proves to be the case, do not feel that you have failed in any way. Perform the ritual, leaving the labrys at the mountain sanctuary. If you do not hear from him in the next few days, do not lose hope. In performing the ritual, you are opening the door for reception at any time."

She placed the labrys within my two hands, wrapping her hands around mine and holding firmly. "I wish you peace through this journey," she said, closing her eyes and concentrating.

"Thank you," I said, when it was clear she had completed her prayer.

I took the labrys from her. It was heavy with power. I felt intimidated by it.

"One more thing," she said, "before I tell you the ritual."

"Yes," I said. "What is it?"

"If you feel very strongly that you want to know someone, then it is certain that you do know him and have known him all along. It is not a stranger you seek."

I looked at her. "I do not understand," I said. "Could you explain further?"

"What I have just said will become clear to you as you perform the ritual."

I took the labrys home and stood it up inside the libation hole in the floor of my room. "In placing this labrys where I live, it is my wish to recollect," I said, carrying out the first part of the ritual.

That night I wrapped it in cloth and placed it under my mat, at the place where my head would rest.

In slumber, I received a dream. It was brief, yet vivid and haunting, the kind of dream you feel inside of you. There was a man. He had long, thick, curly, dark hair hanging over a strong, muscular torso. His stature was short and compact, bursting with energy and vibrance. His bare back was reddened from the sun. He stood in the sea, at the place where the water breaks herself into fierce crashing waves before riding to shore. He held a woman in his arms, lifting, almost throwing, her into the air each time a new wave came. She laughed heartily, hanging on to his neck and shoulders. Her dress was wet and dragging into the water, her long hair hung in wet strands around him. It was Sheena—a younger Sheena—with a lightness about her I had never known. The more she laughed, the larger his smile grew, the higher he tossed her into the air. Finally they tired, settling into an embrace—noses touching, eyes locked-until he plunged them together under the waves.

These are my parents, I acknowledged to myself within the dream. Of this joy was I conceived. Yet when I woke up it was the Sheena of my dream I was more compelled by than the person I assumed to be Marcelles.

When I met Sheena in the central court in the morning, I immediately felt it—a reserved air she carried, a sort of tension. After a meal we began our journey toward the peak sanctuary. It was a long hike, consuming the whole day, to there and back. We left early.

I had been told to carry the labrys in an upright position the whole way, never letting the blades hang down. When the priestess had told me this I did not think it would be difficult but the longer we walked, the heavier it became. I was allowed to lean it upon my shoulders, which I did, but even that began to feel cumbersome. I longed to simply let the blades fall toward the ground. It would have been so much easier, but I knew I could not. I tried not to think about it, distracting myself with other thoughts.

Sheena had smiled tenderly when I had shown her the labrys. She took it into her hands, rubbing gently the engravings with her fingers. She was not at all surprised. She had known the priestess would give me a gold one.

She said little on our walk, remaining involved with the thoughts inside her own head. She held the small copper labrys between her thumb and the palm of her hand, pushing its sharpened edges against the skin on the inside of her thumb.

The priestess was right. Marcelles had been with me all along. My mother carried him with her.

"Is he near you often?" I asked, as we sat and ate a bit.

"He has not gone far," she paused, looking at me. "He seems to be waiting for something." The wind blew her hair around her face which was worn and thin. I knew what it was, what had taken away her lightness: it was sorrow, it was longing, it was loss.

"What things people carry inside them," I said to her.

"Yes," she said, looking down at her own hands. "What things."

It was such a relief to finally reach the peak. My arms were aching under the weight of the golden labrys. I only wanted to be free of it. The mountain sanctuary stood before us. It was a small, three-walled room built into a cliff at the peak of the mountain, facing east. It had a facade and a roof similar to the one of the Center and the marina. Inside, on many levels, were wheels and spirals with holes in them in which to place an offering, a libation, or a labrys.

"In placing the labrys at the mountain peak," the priestess had said, "we are honoring the cycles of life, knowing what once was still is, and will be again. We also send a wish for ease in the transformation for the person we are remembering, regeneration of the spirit, and lastly, we open ourselves to communication. These things you think of as you place the labrys inside the mountain sanctuary, in honor of your father."

We found two holes beside each other in one of the central wheels. We placed them, one at a time, first raising them high in the sky to adore Her. We stood looking at them, side by side. It was cold; the wind blew at us, pressing. Sheena put her arm around me. I moved in close to her. I looked up at her face, strong and wise—happy to have found her.

The way back would be easier: empty-handed and lighter.

 **CHAPTER 4**

In Minoa, there was the belief that each person has a purpose, something they alone can uniquely offer. As a flower offers naturally beauty, nectar and fragrance; as a tree offers easily shade, fruits, feasts of green for the eyes; so too a person has that which wants to flow through her.

It was each person's job to discover what that was and, in that capacity, serve the community in which she lived. Each contributing of themselves in this manner keeps a community harmonious and balanced.

Many of the mothers in our block worked in the Center. We would walk them to the Center in the mornings and then proceed down the white brick pathway that led to Dolphin Cove. We would spot the dolphins while we were still up on the hill overlooking the cove as they followed the fishing boats returning from their early morning trips. Jumping, arcing, they almost flew through the air. We would run down the narrow dirt pathway overgrown with tall grasses and wildflowers until we reached the shore. Some days we would go into the water and swim with the dolphins. They would let us ride on their backs or hold on to their fins while they pulled us along.

The dolphins have taught us many things: how to swim, how to touch, but, most importantly, it is through the dolphins that we learned how to breathe. Through practice of the "dolphin release" and the "dolphin fourfold" breath, we have made many important discoveries. The breath is taken in deeply, held for a period of time, then released in one big exhalation followed by three shorter ones. This rhythm is continued until all of the breath is renewed inside the body. This breath and variations upon it have been found useful for many purposes: for calming and awakening energy, for assistance in the trance state, for women bringing forth a child and, general, prolonged health.

It was hot and sunny the day I learned of my own gift, a day like most others. We walked our mothers to the Center in the morning. They gathered in the court in front of the entrance, visiting. Danelle tugged at my skirt. "Come on," he said. "Let's go."

I turned to follow him down the white stone path which led to the crest of the hill above Dolphin Cove. That was when I heard it.

"Don't go in the water today," the voice said, "even though the dolphins beckon."

It was not my voice, but strangely another voice inside my head. I knew it was not my voice because it had a different intonation from my own. It seemed the voice of an older person. A confident, wise voice, followed by a deep internal cramp behind my navel and a fluttering in my chest. I ran down the path with the rest of them, a heaviness in my feet I had not known before.

From the top of the hill we could see the dolphins following the fishing boats, jumping and leaping. The blooming jasmia were scenting the entire island. It was said when the jasmias are in bloom residents of Minoa grow dizzy with the smell of beauty. The water was deep blue with the slightest edging of bright green. The sky was cloudless.

Down on the beach my friends jumped and called to the dolphins, who in turn danced and twirled themselves around in the water, squealing in playful delight. They were inviting us in.

"Let's go," Danelle said, stripping off his clothes.

"No," I heard myself say, before I had even decided that I would. "Don't go in the water today, even though the dolphins beckon," I said, repeating what had been said earlier inside my own head.

The children looked at me with a question across their faces. Thela came and stood close to me.

"Please, don't go in," I said. "I'm scared." I sat myself down in the warm sand and hugged my knees close to my chest. Thela sat down beside me.

The others stood stunned, looking from me to the dolphins and back again. The dolphins had begun to sing, their high-pitched sounds echoing off the cove rocks. No one went in the water though it was clear all wanted to. The sun beamed down upon us. Danelle put his clothes back on and looked out at the water, hands on his hips. The wind blew, carrying jasmia through the air. I was about to explain why I had said it; I felt I owed them some sort of explanation. Someone began to shout. It was Giorgio. He was standing at the edge of the water. He screamed until it became louder and louder, his thick black curls jumping in the air. Finally we heard his words. "Shark, shark!" he was saying. "Angry looking shark!" He turned and shouted toward the dolphins, "Go quickly! Shark! Shark!" The dolphins swam swiftly away, the shark close behind.

"No one must go in the water today," Giorgio said, approaching us. "You were right, Aureillia. How did you know?"

"The voice," I said meekly. "The voice told me, up by the Center."

"A voice?" Danelle said. "What voice? What are you talking about?"

"A voice in my head. The voice of another inside my head."

Danelle's eyes blazed at me with intensity. I lowered mine from his, looking at the sand in confusion.

"We must warn people," Giorgio interrupted. "Helen, you go to the village. I'll go to the marinas. Danelle, you take the Center."

They dispersed themselves quickly. Thela sat next to me. We stayed seated on the beach for a long time, listening to Mother Sea meet the rocks of the cove. It was the time of the rounded moon, making the sound of their joining even more intense. It was not unusual for the dolphins to be so excited or to even see a shark among us at this time. We had always been taught to take care upon entering the water at this phase of the lunar cycle. The cove was empty. No children came; word must have spread.

"You know what this means, don't you?" Thela said. "Your hearing voices?"

"Yes," I said, staring at the place where the sky met the water far in front of me.

"I know the perfect place," she said, standing up and holding her hand out to me. "Come on."

I followed her for a long while along the rocks which line the craggy part of the shore. My body felt awkward and off balance. I was tired and would not have known what to do with myself. I was thankful to be trailing behind her not knowing where she was leading me.

Thela had been blessed with the beauty of Sheena. Her hair was thick and wavy, black as the hair on a black cat. Her eyelashes were the same, even holding water on them while swimming. As I followed behind her, I admired the place where her dark back was stained white from the sea water, where her low-cut white dress brushed against her protruding shoulder blades. As well as beautiful, she was extremely strong. Her legs were muscular and her arms large. This was a difficult trail, yet she stumbled not once.

Thela was a chanteuse. She had been recruited recently by the Center chanters. Her voice was strong and vibrant, happy and soulful.

We had to jump from rock to rock over swift moving waters, climb up one side of a steep boulder and slide down the other side on our buttocks; edge our feet slowly across a narrow ridge on the side of a cliff. A few times my foot slipped, nearly tossing me into the tumultuous waters below me. I was quite relieved when Thela finally turned to me and said, "We made it."

"To where?" I asked, short of breath, my dress hanging wet against me.

"To the cave of Medena," Thela pointed to a dark opening in the cliff above us.

I had never been to the cave of Medena, Mother of Darkness. I was surprised Thela knew the way. I had heard people speak of it, describe this long, treacherous walk we had just undertaken as the only way to get to it.

As soon as we entered Her dark mouth, I knew Thela was right. This was the perfect place. The light behind us was swallowed up quickly inside the tunnel. Groping the walls with our hands, we tried to feel our way forward into the sudden blackness. Thick humid air pressed against me as I pushed forward slowly, my fingers tracing the many bumps of the cool, damp cave walls.

The darkness, so shocking and complete, made me keenly aware of my physical body, the places where my skin met the air, the hairs rising in wonder. I was aware of the sockets of my non-seeing eyes, the tip of my nose, the bones of my cheeks. The thoughts that were rambling around inside my head became louder, reaching a crescendo before softening, dissipating as their focus settled intently upon getting to where I did not know I was going. After we struggled for some time, the darkness dissolved into grayness, then into a weak yellow light which led us to a large round opening inside the cave: the shrine room.

Through a small hole at the top of its domed ceiling came a light, at first blazing white brightness before dispersing itself into dimness upon the many stalactites which grew down from it. At one end of the room spread a long altar covered with offerings. Beside it stood a tall pillar—the Medena—its base encircled with stones.

"It is so beautiful, Thela," I said. "How is it that you came to know the way here?"

"My mentor brings me here to practice my chanting," she said. "The first time, I could not sing. I was so overwhelmed by the magic. I did not want to disturb it. But then my mentor taught me about the properties of sound. She told me that my chanting could actually have a cleansing effect upon this space. 'Never be afraid to sing,' she said to me. 'If it is done out of pure desire, it is always a healing thing.'"

"Come," Thela continued, taking my hand and leading me toward the altar. She placed the jasmia blossoms she had brought upon it. I placed the shells I had brought beside the large white flowers. We sat silent time before the pillar. Then Thela stood up, and, positioning herself directly under the funnel of light, began to chant. Her voice echoed and bounced within the walls of the shrine, making the power of it only more evident. It was clear to me why her mentor brought her here. I lay against the floor, spreading my arms wide on either side of me, letting the vibrations bounce upon my wide open chest. The sound surrounds me, my body's vibrations rising to meet it. I become one with the sound.

The sound was still vibrating within the shrine after Thela had finished singing. It swam through the air tinkling upon the long legs of the stalactites, flowing upon the circular currents of air in the shrine, a low humming. I stared up at the bright pinhole of light in the ceiling above me, wondering.

"I want to show you something else," Thela said.

We exited the shrine through a different tunnel from the one we had followed in. Darkness came swiftly and seemed more severe than it had before. I stumbled along clumsily, stubbing my toes on the grooves and bumps of the wet surface of the floor beneath me.

"Shhh. Stop," Thela said, holding out her hand so that I met it. "Listen."

I stopped and closed my eyes. There was a loud, rhythmic, whistling echo inside the tunnel. It was this which had been disorienting me.

"Follow the sound," Thela said.

I did as she said, focusing on the sound and moving toward it. The way became easier. The whistling grew louder and louder until it became a scream. When it was most intense, Thela held my arm firmly.

"Take great caution," she said, leading me slowly forward. Astoundingly sudden, the tunnel widened to daylight. On a narrow ledge we stood, surrounded by the deep brown waters of Mother Sea. Emerging from her depths were tall stones with birds perched upon them. In one of the stones, Mother Sea had carved a hole through which her waters passed with every pulse. It was from this that the whistling sound came. The ledge was covered with an assortment of exquisite shells. Thela and I gathered many of them into the large pockets of our dresses. We often sat by the fire in the evenings stringing shell necklaces together. This would be one of those evenings. We sat dangling our legs over the ledge into the water. When the water was as high as we were and our stomachs were rolling with hunger, we decided it was time to walk back.

*   *   *

That evening the recruiter from the temple of the Snake Goddess came to see me.

"Oh, yes," she said when she saw me. "You have a few more years, but there will be no stopping you. You are definitely a priestess of the Snake Goddess."

She put her hands on my shoulders and looked into my face. Her face was small, the brown skin was dry and wrinkled, making her nose seem large. She wore a purple cloth wrapped around her head. It covered her hair completely, leaving her piercing black eyes exposed. I knew very little about what went on inside the temple of the Snake Goddess. I knew that all knowledge was passed from the Snake to Her priestesses: knowledge of other planes of existence, knowledge of things to come, messages from those already taken back and information on other times and places.

At Snake Goddess celebrations, Her priestesses shared what Snake had taught them. These teachings were then taken and passed through the teachings of the Center. No one was allowed inside the temple of the Snake Goddess except for Her chosen priestesses.

I knew that Snake had created all that was: the earth, the waters. It was She who filled the skies around us. I knew that from Her ever-changing skin we were born, and into Her all-encompassing mouth we would return someday, to be shed again and again into new forms.

I knew nothing about what it meant to be a Snake priestess. I had heard it whispered that some women did not survive the initiation, that Snake priestesses lived very short lives, that very few brought forth children. From what I had observed on my own, it was clear that if they did survive to an older age, they were always among the wise women on the council of elders. I also knew that though this recruiter looked old she did not have on her many years.

Though it was a great honor to have your daughter selected by the Snake Goddess, that night my mother wept for me.

* * *

The next day, Barbara came to see me. She was a stunning, regal woman with wavy auburn hair flowing down beneath a crown of snakes. She wore a white, ankle-length, sleeveless dress belted tightly around her waist. Gold armbands of snakes traveled up and down her arms to cover fresh bites.

"Last night, I had a dream about you," she said, "that means it is I who am to mentor you. I shall guide you through your apprenticeship in the temple when the time comes."

She squatted down to my height, her eyes studying me. I had never seen a kinder face. There was a pink light shining off it. She had deep green eyes and an eloquent nose, curving ever so slightly at the end. Pain was there as well, in the slight creases beside the eyes, and in the tiny lines on her forehead. I pulled away from her.

"I am not ready," I said instinctively, though I did not know what I meant.

But she did. "Of course you are not," she said. "And don't try to be, either." Her voice was strong and confident. "Go and enjoy yourself for as long as you can."

She stood up and looked around. "It is my obligation to present myself to an apprentice as soon as I discover who she is. That is the only reason I have come. You will know when you need me. I will be waiting, in the temple, of course."

She leaned her face up toward the sun for a long time. "So nice to be outside," she said, smiling. Her lips were lavender. Her teeth were straight and white.

"Enjoy your youth," she whispered urgently into my ear after kissing me on both cheeks. Then she walked away. My eyes followed her down the path leading away from my block—the path leading back to the Center—until they could not follow her anymore. I had never seen one person possess so much grace; it was evident even from behind. The walkway overgrown with the plant life around it, trees bending above it—the sun shining herself between them—a tall woman walking upon it, back as straight as any temple pillar, the crown on her head never once faltering.

* * *

"A Snake priestess?" Danelle said the next day, digging a stick into the dirt. He drew one S, then another S, then he connected them, forming a snake.

We were sitting up on a hill overlooking the blue sea, the endless sky. The jasmia smell was everywhere, encompassing us. I could have breathed its earthy, musky fragrance forever. I took deep, long sips of it. Everyone had been told to stay out of the water. Another shark had been spotted.

"There must be rough water somewhere," Danelle said, "driving the sharks in. The waters look calm from here."

We had been picking berries and eating them. My stomach was very full. I lay back and put my hands upon it, closed my eyes, and let the hot sun shine upon my face. "Snake priestesses are strange," Danelle said.

In my mind was the image of Barbara, walking away. "I don't think so," I said. "I think they are wonderful."

"If they are anything like the sculpture in the temple," Danelle said, "then yes, I suppose you are right. They are wonderful."

"You saw the sculpture inside the temple?" I said, sitting up. I was shocked.

"Yes. As an apprentice in sculpture I was shown all the major works on the island."

"Oh, my goodness, Danelle! You must tell me about Her. I simply have to know. Please. What is it like inside there?"

"You know I cannot, Aureillia. It would not be fair to you. I should not have even told you that I saw it."

"Oh, but you must! You have to! I simply have to know!"

"I am so sorry, Aureillia. I made a promise to my mentor. I cannot break it. You must be able to form your own opinion when the time comes."

"Oh, Danelle. Why must you be so conscientious?" I said, slapping my hand against the dry dirt, bringing up dust. I looked into his eyes but he looked away quickly.

"Jasmia moon," he said.

"What?" I said loudly. I had heard him but did not understand why he said it. He did not respond to me but remained quiet for some time, looking out to the water, thinking. His blond hair was scattered around his face. I had heard people talk about the jasmia moon and how it drove people to crazy acts of passion and intensity. The smell was overwhelmingly seductive.

"Aren't you scared?" Danelle asked when he finally spoke to me again.

"Yes, quite," I answered quickly.

"Of course you are," he said. "I think I am even frightened for you." He smiled at me with such gentleness that all my anger dissipated. He was changing; in another moon he would be initiated into male being. He seemed uneasy with himself of late; worried, confused.

"I'm really quite interested in all of this," he said. "Will you promise to tell me when it happens again?"

"I don't know," I said. "You would not tell me about the temple."

"You have no right to ask me to tell you that. You know that. Please, Aureillia?"

That depends," I said, teasing, "on what you will give me."

"I'll sculpt you another stone. I already know what it shall be."

"All right," I said, laying myself back down upon the dirt. "I promise."

# CHAPTER 5

For me, there would be two initiations. An initiation into female being and an initiation into the temple of the Snake Goddess.

"Becoming a woman is a blessed gift," Metha said. "One must never forget or minimize the greatness of responsibility that this gift brings." Metha was a priestess in the temple of Female Being.

We met once a lunar cycle and she schooled me in the knowledge and skills I would need when I became a woman. It was she who would lead me through my initiation, assist me in bringing forth a child, and any other passages that come with being a woman. Metha would be my guide for life.

"We create and nurture the children of this earth," she continued. "The kind of world we live in depends on the kind of nurturing our children have received."

We were in the field of sacred herbs. Their flowers spread purple, pink, and white around us. Metha was teaching me which herbs to mix together for controlling fertility.

"For most women," she said, "controlling fertility is an important aspect of their life, but even more so for a Snake priestess. For you, the closest attention must be given to the preparation and administration of your tonics. There can be no mistakes or surprises for a woman on the venom."

"Tell me about the venom, Metha."

Metha looked at me. Her deep ebony skin reflected the sunlight. Her thick black hair was held back from her face by a sash of purple silk. She wore a matching deep purple dress. She had three children of her own, all older than I. I could see that she was trying to decide whether or not she should tell me about the venom.

"Your Snake priestess mentor will school you well in the ill effects of the venom," she said, in a very level manner. "As for fertility, I can tell you what we have learned. We have learned that the venom travels to every part of a woman's body, even the womb and sacred waters which house the child within her for ten consecutive lunar cycles. We are not sure whether it is the venom itself or the visions, which the becoming child sees and cannot process. Either way, the child is unable to live. There have been strange variations reported in the expelled fetuses. No," she said, shaking her head in dismay. "A Snake priestess' womb is no place for life becoming."

Tears had welled up in my eyes, surprising me. Metha put her arms around me and held me close to her. Her body was round and cushiony soft, immensely comforting.

"You are making a great sacrifice on behalf of your community," she said. "Snake priestesses are very important to us. We have learned immeasurable amounts about so many things from women of your gift."

She held me away from her with my two wrists in her hands and looked at me. "There are many children who need much love. Being a mother is so much more than bringing forth a child."

*   *   *

The day my first blood came, Thela and I were out for a walk, collecting shells along the beach. Thela had been initiated and lived in a different block. She spent most of her afternoons practicing in the temple or chanting, so this was a rare afternoon together.

"Oh, look," she said, pointing to my leg, "you must have cut yourself, for you bleed."

I looked down to see my leg stained with blood. I went into the water and washed it off but found no cut. "Look, Aureillia," she said again, later on. "It bleeds still."

"But there is no cut, Thela," I said, looking down upon my leg, "and it is in a different spot. What is happening?"

"Could it be?" Thela said, a smile covering her face. We followed the trail of blood back to its place of origin, which indeed was my sacred spot.

"Two moons away from womanhood, my darling sister," Thela said, very excited. "You will love being a woman."

"Will I, Thela?" I said. "I am so very nervous." "Oh, yes," she replied. "It is such a rewarding thing to be a woman—to have a natural flow and a rhythm, to be one with the moon. I cannot wait until we can talk about it together, after your initiation."

Thela had been initiated three annums earlier. I remembered seeing a dramatic change in her at the time, and feeling a change in our relationship. There were things she knew which I did not—mysteries.

"This is a big transition in your life," she said to me, putting her fingers through my hair gently. "Girlhood is ending. Go slowly. Life is fleeting."

After we parted, I felt anxious. I decided to go to the Cave of

Mother Sea. In the Cave of Mother Sea there are pools, steaming hot and full of soothing minerals. Sitting within these pools eases tension and anxiety. I had been here many times before with my mother and Thela, but I had never entered Her alone.

The cave was dark and damp. I lit the lamps surrounding the water, removed my clothing, and slipped down into the largest of the bubbling pools. Small, energetic bubbles pushed against my skin persistently, forcing the heat to enter me. When it penetrated my inner being, the heat radiated itself back outward toward my skin until it and the water became one. I closed my eyes and breathed the fourfold breath of the dolphin, leaned my head back, and enjoyed the feeling of dissolving. When I opened my eyes, I was on the roof of the cave looking down at at my own body inside the pool. I had heard people tell of these kinds of experiences inside the Cave of Mother Sea. Until it happened to me, I did not understand. More than scared, I was fascinated. The part of myself that I know of as me was up near that roof: that was me. The part others know of as me was down floating in that pool: she was the stranger. To look at myself like that, to see myself from the outside, was chilling.

Upon re-entry into my body I received a vision: it was me. I was crawling on my hands and knees along the dirt path that leads from the Center toward the Cave of Mother Sea. My face was pale and drawn, my hair long and lifeless. I was inconceivably thin. Deep, dark circles outlined my eyes. I was murmuring something to myself frantically. Danelle came up from behind me and put his arms around me.

"What is the meaning of this, Aureillia?" he asked.

"Oh, Danelle," I said, turning toward him. "I am so tormented. You will never know."

The vision ended with the same suddenness that it had begun. I found myself shivering inside the pool, though I knew the water to be very hot. I climbed out, dressed quickly, and walked to the temple of the Snake Goddess within the Center.

The moment I entered the temple, I was stunned by a strong, pungent, almost rotten smell. Then I saw it, on the left side of the temple: a pit full of snakes. Their skins were differing shades of copper brown and deep red stripes. They slithered and crawled upon each other, bunching up into a corner of the pit. In the center of the pit there was a hearth for use during the rainy season.

The temple's walls, ceiling and floors were painted in a spiraling, intertwining, snakeskin pattern of red and black. Some of the spirals were large and swirling in wide, open arcs. Some were smaller, winding themselves into tight coils. The eye was unable to follow one coil from start to finish, getting led unsuspectingly onto another spiral, lost in the endless pattern of coiling and uncoiling.

Doorways in the back and to the sides of the temple were covered with curtains of black silk. These, together with the mural, gave the feeling of enclosure. High in the wall above the entrance, there were small windows facing out into the central court. Streams of light sliced in through them, interrupting the darkness of the temple.

Though a large room with many people in it, it was extremely quiet. Many women sat upon different colored pillows, some were in quiet conversation, some in meditation. Others were lying down upon straw mats, and a few seemed to be sleeping. Light silk coverings were spread upon them. In the distance could be heard the faint murmuring of the Center chanters. I thought longingly of Thela.

I spotted Barbara from behind, her strong back rising up from a round red pillow. "I've been expecting you," she said before I had fully approached her.

"How did you know?" I asked.

"The voice told me."

"What voice?"

"The voice which speaks to us. The voice of the serpent."

"The serpent? My goodness," I said, "is that who that is?"

"Shhh," Barbara said, bringing her hands together in front of her chest. "Sit," she commanded, pointing to another round red pillow placed across from her.

I sat myself on the pillow and crossed my legs in front of me, like her. The instinctive trust I felt for her helped me to relax. She did not look at me but at a spot on the wall behind me, then she took some deep breaths and released them slowly. I began to breath with her, feeling myself quiet down inside.

"The first thing we learn in the temple of the Snake Goddess," she said, finally, "is to speak softly so as not to disturb apprentices learning or priestesses in trance."

I nodded my head, feeling ashamed at the way I had entered the temple. As though she sensed my feelings, Barbara said, "Most people who enter the temple bring the outside world in with them. It is for this reason that we are so restrictive about who we allow in here. Part of the initiation is learning how to leave those things behind to better interact with the Goddess. Now, tell me—what brings you here today?"

"Just now, down at the Cave of Mother Sea, I had a vision which frightened me."

"What was the nature of this vision?"

"It was me in an absolutely horrifying state, and Danelle. He was trying to comfort me."

"Danelle," she said, not in the form of a question.

"Yes, he's—"

"I know who he is," she interrupted. "You are lucky. Most Snake priestesses do not have a Danelle."

I looked at her. I knew I was not understanding her meaning. "You see," I continued, "I came here because I would like to start my initiation immediately."

"Why is that?"

"Because I am terribly frightened. I do not understand what my vision meant. What could I have been so upset about?"

"Aureillia," Barbara said, leaning close to me where I was able to distinguish that her face was covered with small red freckles. "You must trust that whatever happens to you, you will find the strength to handle it at the time that it happens to you. No sooner. I am not permitted to initiate you until you have been initiated fully into female being. Have you yet received first blood?"

"Today. It is for this reason that I entered the Cave of Mother Sea."

"Congratulations," she said, smiling jubilantly. "That means you shall be coming to me soon. In the meantime, take care upon entering any waters alone. It seems the snakes are anxious to speak with you. It can be very disconcerting if you are not prepared."

Barbara took my hands into her own, so that my hands were upraised inside them. She closed her eyes and said a silent prayer for me. I had never felt toward anyone what I felt toward her—an overwhelming desire to be like her. Would I ever be this calm? Could I ever possess this much wisdom and power? I began to look forward to my future.

Before leaving the shrine, Barbara took me to see the sculpture of the Snake Goddess. She stood on top of a tall altar in the middle of the temple, her back to the entrance. Offerings of shells and pottery were scattered around her. The tiers of her tall hat matched those on her ankle-length skirt. Her breasts were exposed from within a high collared shirt. Within each of her hands, she clutched a copper and black striped snake which she raised to the sky—two strong arms reaching, holding, possessing power. The sculpture was positioned in such a way that the sunlight landed on her from behind, casting a huge, looming shadow in front of her. I do not know which was more powerful, the sculpture or the shadow.

I returned to my room and slept for the rest of the afternoon. I did not go to dinner. Sheena brought some food to my room which I nibbled at anxiously.

I knew I had to tell Danelle; I had promised him so long ago. But I stalled. I dallied. I did not understand why, but it had become difficult for me to be near him. I had become painfully aware of myself around him, overly sensitive to each of my own movements, to everything he said and even more to what he did not say. This awkwardness had led to my avoiding him. I had become very good at it, for weeks now managing it for days at a time.

I stayed in my room until I could not stand it any longer. I knew where to find him: every evening he went to the Cove of Circling Waters to soak his hands in the whirlpool. The work he did was extremely difficult on his hands. The whirlpool helped remove the pieces of dust and stone that became embedded in them.

It was a glorious evening. There was no presence of moon, allowing the stars to show themselves. Even the tiniest speck of a star sparkled brightly.

I saw Danelle from up on the hill. He squatted on a stone, his bare back leaning in toward the waters as he soaked his hands. This sight turned my insides over, heating me up at the core. I felt myself flush and become lightheaded. I wanted to turn and walk away but I knew I could not. I knew I must go to him.

"Danelle," I said, as I approached him.

He stood up and turned to my voice. "Aureillia, I was only now thinking about you. Where have you been hiding yourself? I have not been able to find you." He moved toward me, moisture clinging to the soft blond hairs that covered his bare chest. I backed away from him. I could not breathe.

"What is it?" he said.

"What?"

"Something about you. You look different."

"Do I?" I said, holding my hands to my face. "I received first blood today," I said to the ground, then added quickly, "but that is not what I came to tell you."

"Well," he said, taking my hands from my face into his, "what is it that you came to tell me?"

"I had a vision today," I looked up into his face. It had become thinner, his cheekbones more defined. Deep, vertical creases lined the center of his forehead. I lifted my hand instinctively to touch them. "You must scowl when you work," I said.

He pulled me to him, taking my lips into his warm mouth.

I was so surprised I pulled away and looked into his eyes, which did not look away but deeper into mine. His hands moved from my back up the length of my neck, exploring my face. I leaned myself in toward him, offering him again my mouth.

* * *

"Close your eyes," Danelle said to me one evening.

We were sitting in the sand at dolphin cove.

I closed my eyes and felt him remove my owl pendant and replace it with something else. "Now," he said. "All set."

I put my hand to it before opening my eyes. It was a small figure of a woman, arms upraised. I opened my eyes.

When I looked down I could not believe what I saw: an exact miniature replica of the sculpture of the Snake Goddess I had seen in the temple the other day. Around her waist and between her arms, blending into her garment, was the rope from which she hung around my neck. There would be no need to drill a hole into this one.

"Danelle," I said, sitting up straight. "How did you ever? She is so incredible."

"I made it for you so long ago," he said, "I was so impatient to give it to you. I almost did, so many times. But now is the perfect time and I am so glad I waited."

I put my arms around his neck and kissed him on the ear. I rubbed my face into his soft hair, breathing him in deeply.

"I saw Her the other day," I said. "I went to the temple to see Barbara. She showed Her to me."

"I hear she is quite wonderful."

"Who?"

"Barbara."

"Do you? From whom?"

"She is well spoken of in the Center."

"Yes, she is wonderful. She knows things, things I do not even know about myself."

"They say she is the best there is. You are lucky to have her."

"Yes, I am," I said. "Odd," she said the same thing about you."

"Did she?"

"Yes, she did," I said, relaxing into him. I held the Goddess in my hand. Her strong arms extended up, holding forth her snakes. Her strength was unquestionable.

# CHAPTER 6

All initiations are secret. I did not know what to expect when I entered the moon of the third and most sacred bleeding. Three is the sacred number of the Goddess. When a girl enters her third cycle of bleeding, she meets with her mentor, a priestess from the temple of Female Being. They begin a cycle of initiation.

For one whole moon, I would leave the places and people I knew as a girl. When I returned to them, I would be a woman—one aware of the mysteries of her sacred female being.

I knew that this was an ending as well as a beginning. I had seen the results on other girls who had gone before me, returning at the end of the moon shining differently—another color.

Danelle had also changed greatly after his initiation, of which I would never know. So it was with fear, sadness and much anticipation that I went to meet Metha at the temple.

The temple of Female Being had its own entrance in the lower west wing of the Center. I was not prepared, however, for the hallway—long and dark—seeming to arrive at nowhere as I walked and walked within it. I began to wonder if this was, indeed, the way when I suddenly stumbled down a few steps and landed within the temple.

There were many other girls present, which surprised me at first. I had not realized that we would be initiated together. It took me a while to find Metha, but I was sure this was the temple because the entire room—walls, ceiling and floor—was painted bright red. Carved into the walls, floor and ceiling, underneath the red paint, were the many representations of the butterfly and her counterpart—the sacred labrys. Whenever anything is becoming, the butterfly is present. We were all becoming women and she was here sometimes floating, sometimes flying, curved edges, straight edges: but all underneath, emerging.

Metha was wearing a long red robe that extended down to her ankles. "Aureillia," she said to me when she found me, "welcome."

She led me to stand in line behind other initiates and mentors. I did not know what we were waiting for because what was happening was going on behind a red curtain.

When our turn came, Metha led me through the curtains into a small low-ceilinged room with steps leading into a stone bath. In the center of the water was a deep hearth in which burned a fire, heating up the waters around it. Steam rose from the water. It was difficult to breathe at first. My body released moisture. Metha chanted:

> *In nakedness we are created*
> *In nakedness we create*
> *Stand before the Goddess as She created you.*

I removed my clothing and walked slowly down the steps into the water. It was intensely hot; I could feel it scorching my skin, bringing life to each place that it touched. Its texture was sleek and oily. Herbs floated upon it. The smell of sage and sweet marjoram penetrated my nose and throat, clearing them. The water reached just below my shoulders.

Metha came in behind me. Her breasts, large and round with deep, brown nipples, floated upon the water. She carried a large white shell full of flower blossoms which she tossed into the bath, sending them floating around me. When the shell was empty, she filled it with the steaming water and poured it over my head. She continued the chant:

> *To the maiden*
> *To her youth*
> *To the girl that you are.*

She turned me around three times, holding me by the shoulders, filled the shell again and poured it over my head. The hot water streamed down my face, my hair, and onto my shoulders, before landing back upon itself.

"Emerge from the waters of girlhood now," Metha said. Out of the water, Metha put a robe of red on me.

My skin was warm and tingly from the bath. The robe rubbed against it smoothly. She tied a red scarf around my eyes, blindfolding me, and led me by the arm. I felt us leave the temple and journey down a hallway out of the Center, into the light of day. I was able to see only shades of light and dark flickering above me. After a while I determined it to be the sun breaking through the branches of trees above us.

We walked for some time, the path beneath my feet turning to dirt. When the shadows stopped and there was only light, we halted. I could feel the presence of other people near me by slight murmurings, the rustling of other robes and breathing. After standing for a while in silence with Metha's hand still holding my arm, the slow pulsing of a drum began. Metha led me forward, taking my left hand into hers, and someone else took my right one.

Metha's hand pulled me around into a ring dance. The ring felt wide. The grass was soft beneath my feet. As we circled the voice of a woman coming from the center of the ring began to chant:

"Today you begin to leave girlhood behind
Your girl body changing to that of a woman
A woman's body is ripe with the juices that create
Stand before the Goddess as She created you."

The circle stopped moving. Metha removed my robe.

The hot sun was upon my skin. She stood behind me and hugged me to her so that I felt the smooth material of her robe upon my back, the soft curves of her flesh. She took my hands into hers and placed them on my shoulders. Metha's voice joined in with the chanting:

"Breasts—life giving, nurturing
Absent on the girl
Ever present on the woman
Honor the sacredness of your breasts."

Metha led my own hands with hers down my shoulders until they reached my own breasts. Within each hand I held my breasts, only recently grown upon my body, soft and cool.

"Life giving womb
Sacred birth chamber."

Metha led my hands down to my belly, which they circled, her hands guiding them in a slow, repetitive movement. She chanted:

"Like a flower opening
To the sun's penetrating rays
So does a woman's body open to sacred touch
Feel yourself opening to pleasure."

Metha led my hands down between my legs. With my own fingers she opened me, exploring gently the moist petals and folds. I gasped in wonder, moisture flowed from me. My nipples tingled firm. Metha finished:

"Pleasure, pain and wisdom
These are the essence of female being."

A loud drumbeat sounded, shaking me back to myself. Metha placed my robe back upon me. She turned me around three times before pulling the knot at the back of my blindfold. Light stung my eyes. I was in the sacred grove. Around me was a wide circle of trees and the other initiates and mentors. As I looked at the initiates I recognized in their faces the expression I felt on my own: shocked, flushed and aroused.

* * *

We were required to make the skirt and crown that we would wear to the rounded moon celebration ourselves. The crown was made of red flower petals, to represent sacred bleeding. The skirt was ankle-length, tied at the waist and hanging open in the front. It was to express things from our girlhood that we would be leaving behind as well as things that we hoped to become as a woman. The shirts, which were provided to us, were traditional and ceremonial. They were close fitting, with elbow length sleeves and a deep opening in the front. This opening allowed the shirt to be pulled open around the breasts in sacred gesture.

"In exposing our breasts," Metha said, "we honor our sacred female being, which mirrors Hers in our ability to create from within ourselves life and the fluids that sustain it."

Indeed, at all the festivals, priestesses wore costumes which exposed and accentuated the breasts.

All the initiates slept in the same room. At night I would hear some of the girls sharing each other. I would listen to their pleasuring and I would enter myself and feel the juices move within me.

In the evenings, we would sit around the temple together working on our skirts and crowns. I had never been very skilled at sewing, in spite of the talents of my mother. I was finding this job particularly frustrating and I did not know why. I would sit, with my half-started skirt in my lap, staring at a butterfly carved under the paint, waiting for it to emerge.

One of the initiates, Katya, saw that I was struggling with my work and offered to help me. Katya was to be a bull leaper in the Center games. She had already begun a rigorous, physical training. Her body was firm and taut with energy. She was very excited about her future. She had sewn bulls and leaping human figures all over her skirt. They frolicked and danced around it in excited glee.

"I cannot wait to begin my apprenticeship," she said, her eyes sparking. "This initiation is the only thing standing in my way." I watched her hands as they sewed my skirt with an efficiency and speed I had never before seen.

Katya had spent her youth outside of Knossos. Her mother was a horticulturist specializing in the cross breeding of olives. Katya had grown up among the trees in the groves. She was very taken by Knossos and anxious to move into the Center with the rest of the bull leapers. As we finished the skirt itself, she began to question me about what I was going to sew on it.

I shrugged. "I suppose I will sew my owl pendant and perhaps some dolphins to represent my youth. Oh, and some of my mother's weaving. Perhaps a shell or two."

"Yes, yes," she said impatiently, shaking her head, her thick brown hair swinging. I had told her that before. "But what about the future? What shall you put for the future? That is the fun part."

"I'm not sure," I said. "I'm still thinking about it." One night I was awakened by the presence of someone standing above me as I slept. It was Katya. As I opened my eyes to look at her, she put her hand upon my breast, asking. I reached my hands out to her, welcoming her into my bed.

"I do not understand you, Aureillia," she whispered to me later, as we lay in my bed together. "You know that you shall be a Snake priestess. Why is it that you do not sew snakes upon your skirt?"

"No. I do not want to," I said quickly. "That is not what I wish to become as a woman."

"Silly thing," she said, "that is what you shall become."

"But it is not what I wish for," I said angrily.

"Aureillia, what is it?" she asked, looking into my face.

"I do not know," I said. "I know I shall be a Snake priestess, but I do not feel overjoyed about it like you do about the bulls. When I think of the snakes, I become frightened." A feeling of relief passed over me as I released my tears. It was clear to me that this was why I had been struggling so with my skirt.

"I'm sorry," Katya said, wiping the tears from my face gently. "I did not know that you were feeling that way."

"Neither did I," I said.

"Well, if it is not a Snake priestess that you wish to become, then what is it?"

"I'm not sure," I said. "I can feel it, I can see it, but there are no words for it."

"Try," Katya said. "Close your eyes and say whatever it is that comes to your mind."

I closed my eyes, moving myself closer to Katya's body so that our edges met. "She is strong," I said. "Strong, yet graceful. She is firm. Firm, yet delicate. She is dark and deep and mysterious. Her wings—that's it," I said, opening my eyes. "A bird. It is a bird."

"Feathers," Katya said, smiling big.

For days we wandered together, gathering feathers. We gathered feathers of all shapes, sizes, and colors. Together we sewed them to my skirt, each holding a different end on our lap, the skirt spreading between us. When it was finished, it was perfect. The feathers gave it the earthy, yet mystical feeling I had been looking for. I did not know what it meant, but it was exactly what I had wanted.

* * *

Metha wakes me up in the darkness. She leads me again to the ritual bath.

"As the moon grows in the night sky," she says, "so inside a woman grows a moon, filling up with ripe roundness, ready to receive. At the time of the rounded moon is found the height of passion and fullness."

It is time for the rounded moon dance. Lamps are lit around the water, which smells of jasmia blossom. The light reflects within its blackness. I enter its depths, warm and welcoming in this cool night air. Quietness surrounds us. Pouring water over my head, Metha chants:

> *"Sacred pleasure*
> *Divine transcendence*
> *Sacred union*
> *Rounded completion*
> *Honor thy fullness*
> *Become one with the moon."*

She helps me on with my skirt and fixes the crown upon my head before blindfolding me. The feathers rustle upon my skirt as I walk, holding her hand in mine firmly. The way is the same as last time except for the darkness and the fragrant soft night air, warmer outside the Center than within it.

When we stop walking I assume the we are once again in the sacred grove. I can feel the presence of many people. There is heat, which must be coming from a fire. A drum beat begins. I can hear dancing happening in front of me. It is men. They chant, letting us know there are men here. Metha places each of my hands into those of the initiates on either side of me. She stands behind me, her hands upon my waist. "These are priests from the temple of Male Being," she says. We move in a circle. The heat from the fire pushes against the front of me. My breasts, my skirt, my face are burning from it.

We stop and circle the other way. Metha's hands are upon my shoulders. When the circle stops again she whispers into my ear, "The blindfolded one is the girl who knows not her female being. When it is clear you have passed from girlhood into womanhood, I shall remove it."

She takes my hands out of the hands of the initiates. They are replaced by the hands of two others. These hands are larger: the hands of men. I can smell that these are men. There is a strong smell of coriander on either side of me. We spin circles again. The circle is widening, holding more people. It moves faster, as we spin, stop, spin again, stop. I am extrememly hot. The dancing stops, hands let go of my hands. I am dizzy, spinning around inside my head. A priest takes my arms into his two hands which begin to explore me. My body responds, moving toward him. I pull the two sides of my shirt open, pleasuring myself upon my breasts as he travels inside the opening of my skirt, his sacred limb pushing against my legs as I open to him, my hips widening as he enters me. I am surprised at first by the thickness of himself but his thickness opens me as I move myself upon him, wanting to better feel him, wanting him more inside myself. I sway and rock upon him. I sink and dig in this dance, dancing up and down as he enters me. My swelling self wraps around him, absorbing him into me deeper more deeply until I surrender my sacred liquid to him in gushing rapture. The blindfold falls. I am face to face with the moon's white fullness in the sky above me.

*   *   *

"With the rounded moon comes the full opening to the light," Metha said to me three days after my full moon dance. "The expanded knowing of the physical life. With the dark moon comes the knowledge of darkness. Within one moon a woman experiences all three aspects of herself: swelling and filling up with sacred juices, rounded fullness, and then, diminishment into darkness. In darkness is the wisdom of the serpent. As the serpent sheds her skin and is reborn, so a woman sheds her inner skin in her bleeding time.

"Women on the venom as well as elder wise women keep their skin within, since the Snake desires to speak with them.

"Women creating another keep the skin within for ten moon cycles. It takes ten snake skins to make a human child."

I was learning which herbs to use during my bleeding time: thyme to ease any discomfort and sage as a relaxant. I would not have many blood cycles during my time as a Snake priestess. The venom, together with the herbs used for controlling fertility, help the woman keep the blood within.

"No less than twenty-six moon cycles after your last intake of venom you may begin to think about conceiving a child," Metha said to me one day.

"If and when the time comes that you carry a child within you, it is I who shall guide you and assist you in bringing forth. Do not forget this: twenty-six moons."

• • •

It was morning when Metha woke me up for my third and final ritual. I had been fasting for two days. She brought me a cup of mint tea. I felt its warm liquid glide through my empty body. She led me to the ritual bath. Pouring water over my head, out of a dark shell this time, she chanted:

> *"Great Goddess guide her*
> *Through the darkness*
> *Toward the light*
> *Into wisdom."*

A black robe was placed upon me, a black blindfold was tied around my head. I could see nothing from under this blindfold, not even shades of light and dark. Metha walked me out of the temple and again out of the Center walls. We walked for a short distance and then she stopped and turned me around several times, disorienting me. She led me on farther. We had not traveled far.

"Stand before the Goddess as She created you," Metha said to me, for a third and final time. She removed all my clothing except for the blindfold. Before removing that she led me farther. I could feel that I had entered a doorway. There was stone beneath my feet. She removed my blindfold but it did no good because the place where I was had no light. I could not even see Metha, though I knew that she was standing right in front of me. Her hands found mine and held them. "In order to become, one must pass through the darkness alone. Take this for your journey," she said, handing me a small cloth bag. "In it you will find all the things that you need." I took the bag to me.

"Now, be on your way," she instructed.

I stood in an absolute daze. "My way?" I said. "What could possibly be my way?"

"Shh—absolutely no talking," she whispered, and then she was gone.

I tried to follow after her, but bumped into a wall hard with the end of my nose. There was no where to go but the other way. I turned and began to walk. Stretching my arms out, I could feel walls on either side of me as though I were in a narrow hallway. The hallway would suddenly end and I would have to feel around for what seemed like far more than four directions before I found another path that led somewhere. I would follow that for a while until I bumped into another wall. This continued for a long time, me walking and twirling and feeling and turning. I was very tired. I sat down and took a few deep breaths, releasing deeply. The cool stone against my naked body chilled me. I pulled my knees up to my chest and fell asleep. I don't know how long I was asleep. I awoke suddenly from a dream.

There was a white dove soaring over the open plains leading away from the Center toward Moon Mountain and Her sacred caves. As she soared and glided I could hear the wind against her sailing wings. It was very peaceful. It was as though I was flying with her. She was pure gentleness.

I sat for a while trying to orient myself inside this darkness. I began to feel around in the cloth bag that Metha had given me. I put my hand upon something that felt like a small loaf of bread. I confirmed this by holding it up to my nose and smelling it. That was when my fingers felt a marking, a sort of design imprinted upon it. I moved my fingers upon it to try to read it. They traced a circle within a circle within another circle. A labyrinth. I stood up swiftly, not being able to contain the fierceness of my heartbeat in a seated position. The realization that I was inside the sacred labyrinth of the Center that I had heard so many tell of sent shock waves through me. Panic overwhelmed me at the thought of being trapped inside it for days, turning around inside the same hallway over and over thinking I was getting somewhere. I began to walk nervously this way and that, bumping my head into one wall, turning and bumping into another, and then another. I reached out in front of me and could only feel wall around me. I was boxed into the smallest possible square, surrounded by cold hard stone. I spun and spun and in my spinning I dropped my bag and heard the contents of it spilling and rolling away. I jumped quickly to the ground to try to recover them, feeling around upon the stone floor on my hands and knees. I could not breathe. Never in my life had I known such darkness. I foolishly kept my eyes open trying desperately to see. Defeated, I lay down upon the floor. That was when I heard it: a voice or a sound, seeming to come up from below the stone, from the earth itself. I turned my head so that my ear was upon the stone, to better hear the sound that was muffled as it made its way through the stone.

"All wisdom lies in darkness," it said. "In the closing of eyes one is able to see."

I closed my eyes. I breathed the dolphin breath. I reached forward and found the opening. The only way out of this corner I was stuck in was to crawl out on my hands and knees. I could feel the stone above me brushing against the top of my back. I crawled along, finding first my empty bag, then the loaf of bread, which I tucked into the bag, deciding to save because I may need it more desperately later. Next on the floor was a tiny goatskin full of perfectly cold, clear water of which I took one sip and saved the rest for later: a small labrys which felt to be carved out of ivory; and a tiny vial of olive oil, for what I knew not. These I returned to my bag. I put the bag around my neck and slung it over my back.

I crawled along the floor, feeling my knees and the palms of my hands begin to bleed. I was finding my way much more easily on the ground. I crawled and crawled. In some places the ceiling got so low above me that I had to lie down flat and slither along like a snake. In these places I could feel that the surface beneath my breasts, belly and legs was a polished, smooth, sensuous marbled stone. Lying there like that, slithering along, I was more completely in touch with my senses than I ever had been before. I could feel everything that came into contact with my body, even a slight change in the temperature around me. I could smell the bread in my bag and the scent of my body as they met the air. I could hear the minutest piece of dust falling off the ceiling above me. When I reached an opening, I let myself stand up and stretch. I ate my bread and drank my water. I spread the olive oil upon my sore knees and palms. I sat down, resting my head against the stone before moving on again. Then I heard the chirping of what seemed to be an enormous number of birds; a frenzied series of chirping, whistling, clicking and fluttering of wings. I had never heard such a thing. As I crawled toward the noise they turned into words and phrases, all at the same time, all speaking to me at once. I shook my head to hear better. I was able to distinguish some of the phrases being repeated:

> *"listen to me*
> *listen to me*
> *look to the light and you shall see*
> *in the darkness*
> *lean on me*
> *look with your listening*
> *with your listening hear"*

I followed the voices until they turned into screams when, as though from nowhere, a white more bright than a light, a light more bright than white came shining down upon me like rain. Above me was a wide opening through which light came pouring in. Around me spread a wide circle, a shrine, at one end of which stood an altar. The altar was full of small, carved labyrses like the one Metha had given me inside my cloth bag. They stood tall and proud—a testament to the many who had passed here before me. I took mine out of my bag. Indeed it was ivory, as I had thought it was. I placed it in one of the holes on the top of the table. I raised my arms above me triumphantly. I had arrived.

*　　*　　*

The time for blindfolds was over. Metha led me, eyes open, to the Red Grotto. I had seen women disappear into it at intervals all my life. I had known it had something to do with one of the many mysteries of being a woman. I had never imagined such a beautiful place could exist. We walked down a grassy path until we reached a clearing where there were many women gathered: some resting, some chatting quietly. When I approached with Metha, they all jumped up excitedly and came to greet me. They took my hands and led me to a waterfall in which they washed me with deliciously fragrant herbs, taking special care of the places that were scratched and bruised, after this they put a warm red robe around me and led me into the grotto. Inside were many lamps lit around the edges of the water. Many women sat in silent time or lay dreaming upon the ledges.

"During the bleeding time the Goddess desires to speak with women," Metha whispered, "so it is that they come to the red grotto, to better listen."

I slept for a long time until I was awakened by a woman I did not know. She helped me up, placed a crown of white flowers upon my head, and led me to a banquet feast that had been set up outside in the grassy clearing. Sheena, Thela, and Hypia were present, along with the other bleeding women of the grotto. We feasted on flatbread, olives, goat cheese, and grape wine. Only initiated women were welcome here. Now, I was one of them.

*　　*　　*

I walked back to my life the same way I had left it a moon earlier—alone. Everything was the same: the same path, the same trees, the same Center, the same sea. Yet all was different. I had never seen any of it before. People saw me for the first time also. They noticed a different person among them. I walked slowly, cherishing this peace inside me, this knowing, this thing burned down, polished and exquisite. The summer winds blew hard against me, my dress blowing viciously around my legs as I stood looking at the sea, feeling the wind, for it was the first wind I had ever felt and it was the first sea I had ever seen and it was fine and it was perfect.

Back in my room I was welcomed by vases of fresh flowers and a new blanket from Sheena spread upon my bed. I lay down and listened to the sounds of my block and the people in it. I smelled the smell of my bed and I reveled in it, for it was the first time and it was new and clean.

I woke up to Danelle's face shining like a sun down upon me. When I began to speak, he put one finger over my lips. "Say nothing," he said. "Follow me."

I followed him innocently, looking around, for I had never been anywhere. All was a wonder. I looked at this man I had never known. I admired his broad shoulders and small, tight buttocks. I adored the back of his head and wondered over his feet. When we reached the top of the hill, he took my face into his hands and kissed me for the first time. I kissed him back and tasted his delicious berry lips and almond tongue. When we shared each other it was sacred and it was pure, for it was the first time, and I knew I loved this man even though I had only just met him.

PART II

# CHAPTER 7

At first I found myself quite ill at ease with the snakes. Though I fed them through a tube, my hand pulled away involuntarily when they got near it. Though their mouths were tied shut as they crawled upon me, my whole being tightened stiff with terror.

Barbara assured me that it was normal to feel afraid at first. She said it took a long time to come to "know" the snakes. "Her wisdom is only for those She deems worthy," she said, "so it is that She makes Herself unapproachable."

I would lie unclothed upon a woven mat on the floor of the temple, waiting. Barbara would choose a snake from the pit for me to lie with. After tying its mouth shut, she would place it upon me.

The first few times I lay there stiff and scared as the snake slithered slowly upon me, each hardened scale slightly scraping the soft smoothness of my belly, my breasts, the backs of my legs.

"Their skin is where they store their magic," Barbara said, on her knees beside me, calmly observing. "To get to know their skin you must feel the coarseness of its many layers against your own. So wisdom is acquired, one layer at a time."

If one began to slither away she would gently guide it back, placing it again upon me and adjusting it with two hands. She had no fear of them and handled them with great authority. Like the sculpture, she was able to hold one in each hand, their mouths free, and not be bitten by them.

"This is the quality of an initiated Snake priestess," she said. "Mutual respect and understanding between herself and the snakes. Only on these terms may a woman receive and process sacred information."

Though she had aged since I first met her, Barbara's beauty had not faded. She wore her long hair in a thick braid trailing down her back; dark red, brown, and golden strands shining separately or together in deep auburn. Her face was at once strong and gentle, with a nose that curved ever so slightly at the end, giving her a most compelling profile. The colors she chose for her clothing—soft yellows, deep purples and bright blues—gave her skin a light that seemed to reflect off her face.

"The Snake is sacred to us for many reasons," she said. "First, there is her power of regeneration, which we so admire. Her ability to shed her skin and, in so doing, releasing another, more vital one beneath. The ability to slough off that which has become no longer useful is one of the greatest lessons in Snake medicine. When we allow snake to crawl upon us, when we feed and care for her, we are asking to be released from the fear that blocks the entrance to wisdom. In this release is found the power of transmutation.

"The second is the wisdom of the bite. Through the bite, Snake transmits Her knowledge to us. She is all knowing. She was here in the beginning and so She shall be in the end. Her wisdom is ancient, yet ever forming. Through Snake priestesses She shares Her wisdom, trusting them to handle properly the information She desires to communicate—injecting them slowly with sacred knowledge, one bite at a time."

As the days passed, I began to enjoy the feeling of snake slithering upon me. I began to look forward to her coarse, scratching movements. I would lie with my arms above my head, close my eyes, and focus on the long, heavy body sinking into mine, stretching from below my neck down into my navel, up over my womb, trailing onto my upper thigh. I would concentrate upon the places where our beings met, my heat becoming hers as the pores of our skin opened to one another in gaping rapture.

Slowly I began to earn my armbands. The golden, twisting, two-headed snakes I had so coveted upon Barbara's arms, became my own.

The first one I earned when I mastered the two-fisted snake stance—the pose captured in the sculpture of the Snake Goddess. We had been practicing for many moons. Still, fear pervaded me. I would not allow Barbara to free the snakes' mouths. I would stand, holding a snake in either hand, raising my arms, face forward, legs firmly rooted, focusing upon the wall of snakeskin in front of me.

"Feel your power," Barbara would say. "Demand respect from them."

But I could not. I could hear her words. I could understand them, but I could not feel them.

My spine would curl, shoulders collapsing, at the feel of the snakes' tight, muscled bodies wriggling within my hands. My fingers would loosen their grip in repulsion, revealing weakness.

Focus. Focus, I would say to myself, staring deeper into the snakeskin wall, but the red and black curling pattern would only remind me of what I held, then the shivers would come.

"It takes time," Barbara would say, seeing my frustration. "Go easy on yourself, Aureillia. This is a long process."

But I could see her thinking, trying to figure out a way to help me.

One day she led me to Mother Sea, to a spot where her waters had stood upon the sand in the morning and since retreated. A place where the earth was made of clay: flat, firm and accepting.

The skies were blue, reflecting deeper blue into Her waters, reaching toward forever in front of me.

"Give me your clothing," she said.

I removed my dress, placing it upon the arm she extended toward me. "Stand upon the sand with your legs slightly parted," she said. "Close your eyes."

I did as she said. The sun beamed down upon my forehead, shoulders and breasts. My feet sank into the clay, which bounced back, warm and moist beneath me. The wind blew, at first softly, then briskly, lifting my hair up before swinging it back against my head and face, pushing against me, challenging my balance.

"What is it that opposes you?" Barbara asked. "The wind," I answered.

"Lift your arms to the sky," she said. "Stand tall to that wind."

I lifted my arms, extending myself upward. My knees bent as my hips lowered toward the ground to better support me.

"Reach for it," Barbara said. "Fight for it."

The wind blew. It forced. It squeezed. I sank my feet deeper into the clay and stretched myself farther upward until I felt the breath enter my ribs. Energy surged in sudden streams from the earth below me up through the soles of my feet, through my legs, into my hips and belly, circling up my back and neck, tittering off the top of my head. The tips of my fingers throbbed with heat. My body beat with its own, loud rhythm, the crashing waves a mere echo of me.

"Open your eyes, and keep your focus on a point in the distance," Barbara said. She reached into the bag she had brought with her and extracted two snakes. "You are strong. You are power. Show them your strength," she commanded. She untied their mouths.

I accepted their gyrating, churning bodies from her hands into mine. I breathed in deeply, lifting them high to the sky, pulling up power from the earth below me until their bodies calmed to stillness in awe of me.

Barbara removed the armband from her left arm, sliding it down her straightened elbow. She slid it up my own, my own self still standing within the clay, waves now crashing into white foaming bubbles around me, power still flowing in waves within me.

Silently, she twisted the golden snakes three times around my arm. I stood admiring the way the gold coils reflected themselves in the bronze of my skin: a head on either end, forked tongue extending, one upon my shoulder, the other at my elbow.

As my understanding of the snakes increased, I was introduced to the venom. Barbara presented me with a small dose in a cup of broth on each event of the rounded moon, increasing the amount with each lunar cycle, allowing my body to build up the powers to transmute the venom.

I would observe in awe as she took hold of a snake, forced its jaw open and squeezed the venom duct until liquid slid down the fang into the collection dish below.

"This too you shall be able to do, in time," she said, sensing my trepidation.

The process of being presented with the broth lasts thirteen lunar cycles. If an initiate survives all thirteen drinks, she receives her second armband, which is worn on the lower half of the right arm. After completion of her initiation ceremony, at which she receives her first bite, she is presented with the crown of golden snakes.

Many initiates do not make it to full priestess. Many grow too ill from the broth and are ordered by their mentors or the Center healers to halt their initiation process. A rare few do not survive.

"We are but vehicles for information," Barbara said. We were in the field of healing herbs. "Never forget that it is the Goddess working through you; using you to tell Her stories. One must heed Her call seriously, always keeping herself strong for Her purposes. It is most important to take good care of the physical body."

I had taken the first two broth presentations without incident and was greatly relieved.

"There is more to life than the temple of the Snake Goddess," Barbara said, looking up at the sun. "If you want your share of it, you must take your tonics diligently. Burdock root is most important for cleansing."

She was right. I had forgotten about the world outside the temple—the world full of color, smells, and sensations. The summer breeze, the singing of the everywhere birds, vast and stretching views for the eyes. Within the temple it was dark. The air was thick with the smell of snakes. Our sleeping quarters were small, windowless rooms deep within the Center. Though I had brought many of my own things into it to try and brighten it, without a lamp lit, even during the day, there was no light. It made one forget about the sun and the light provided by it.

Initiates were not allowed to see anyone from the outside in the time of their training as it was thought that it would prove too distractive. Outside excursions were taken rarely and under careful supervision of the mentor.

Barbara knew about life outside the temple. She had come to her role as a Snake priestess later in life. Her daughter had been taken back by the Goddess at a young age, after a long illness. In her time of mourning, she began to experience visions and voices. So it was that she came to the temple at an older age. Because of this she had had an extensive life outside of the temple. Unlike Snake priestesses who join the temple soon after initiation into female being, having little time to form outside bonds, Barbara had had many when she joined and maintained them within.

She took me with her often to the peak at Mount Juktas to honor her daughter. As we walked the long way together, she would tell me of her life before the temple and of the many places she had traveled to throughout the island.

Most of her evenings were spent among friends. Often she took me with her, stealthily hurrying me out the back corridor, a blanket covering my head to conceal my face. "They are too strict with the initiates," she would remark, leading me quickly down the path outside the Center. "Young women must be allowed time for fun, Snake priestess or not."

To her friends she would introduce me as her friend, so as to not make me or others uncomfortable. I loved to watch how animated she became around her friends, the tension receding from her face as she sang and danced, talked and laughed together with them around the hearth—so very different from her seriousness within the temple.

But all the people, no matter where we went or what we were doing, treated her in the same manner, with the deepest respect and admiration. All sensed something special residing within her, and behaved in a way according to it. This respect they transferred over onto me. I was always very proud to be with her.

I never knew why Barbara was extending such generosity toward me, sharing her friends and her private time with me. I was not able to determine whether it was because she truly thought the rules of the apprenticeship too rigid or whether there was some other reason motivating her.

I did not know what kind of Snake priestess I would become. There were many different types: there were those who provided oracular consultation directly to those who came seeking from Minoa or those who journeyed sacred pilgrimage. There were others who advised the council of elders on matters concerning the community. There were some who received sacred stories, which were passed through the Center teachings in the form of oral myth.

The information Barbara had transmuted had been revealed in closed chamber to the high priestesses and priests. She was unable to reveal to me what it had concerned, since it is their teachings that are the most secretive. Most of her time as a Snake priestess had been spent in the upper levels of the Center, consulting with them. They still came to her often, requesting meetings.

The teachings of the high priestesses and priests were reserved for those chosen. It was never clear to me how one became chosen. Their teachings were a mystery about which Barbara refused to divulge any information.

A Snake priestess discovered her particular function according to the kinds of information the snake chose to transfer to her. Most often a priestess became aware of her function around the time of her third trance dance, at which time she would leave the guidance of her mentor to join her function group. When her physical body had its limit of venom, as determined by her leader and the Center healers, she assumed a new role as mentor to an initiate. The cycle of trance dances was not a long one—a body can only handle so much venom before it becomes toxic again.

Upon the third administration of broth, I was taken ill. I lay in bed sweating and burning from fever for days. Barbara attended to me continuously, bringing broths of burdock root and mushroom, teas of mint and barley, even sleeping beside me through the night. Her diligent attention astounded me. After a full week I was able to get up and slowly walk. I had barely regained my strength when the time had come for another drink. Then I was taken ill again. This cycle continued for three full lunar cycles. I was so weakened from repeated moons of illness followed by another presentation of venom that by the seventh presentation I lay in bed unable to move any part of my physical body except my eyes. When awoke, I was aware of horrifying dreams I had experienced as I slept. Dreams I could not remember clearly, not even pieces, no matter how hard I tried, but whose noises and images haunted me nevertheless.

I had begun to miss everyone in my time of infirmity. I began to think of Danelle and long for him. Every time I closed my eyes, his face appeared, his eyes, looking at me. Melancholy filled my being.

Though I feared and dreaded the full bite of the snake, I was glad the time of initiation was nearing when I could see them all again.

Barbara consulted the Center herbalists. They prescribed me some new tonics and gave her a mixture to add in with the broth. These things helped. I began to gain strength and in the next presentation became ill only briefly, its passing quick and less severe.

The noises I had experienced in my time of illness haunted me. There was a nagging presence inside my head of things I had seen but could not remember. I was intensely bothered by these things, so I asked Barbara about it. "Because there is such a small dose of venom in the broth, the voice of the snake is muted to an inaudible level. One may know of a murmuring but never hear its words. It is very disconcerting, since it never rises to consciousness where one may begin to process it. Try not to let your attention sit upon it, Aureillia. Do not try to understand it. You shall know all soon enough in your cycle of trance dances."

During the days, Barbara and I practiced the trance dance I would perform first at my initiation, then on each event of the rounded moon after that until my cycle of bites was completed. The dance began with me curling myself into the tightest coil possible, knees bent, head down, arms wrapped around my feet, which pulsed from the force of my weight balanced upon them. Slowly, I pushed my chest through my arms into a slither across the floor, raising myself up into another coil. Then I uncoiled myself upward, slowly, slowly, arms rising to the sky, shedding the snakeskin apron around my waist to reveal a brighter, new one underneath. Coiling slowly, back down to the floor, uncoiling up toward the sky, coiling down to the earth until the snake decided to bite me. With each downward coil I was to offer the snake my arm. It was on the arm that a Snake priestess preferred to be bitten. The snake, however, did not always agree to this. Priestesses ended up with bites in the most peculiar places.

The dance required a lot of physical strength and endurance. From my legs, through my belly out through the entirety of my arms, all parts of my body were involved. While performing the dance I was to commune with the snake. I was to ask her to bite me, to share her wisdom, to find me worthy. A chant I repeated within me:

> *"Serpent of wisdom*
> *Most divine one*
> *Present me with the bite that stings*
> *Sacred knowledge in me to sing."*

The time neared for my initiation. I had been in apprenticeship nearly two full annums. In the days leading up to the ceremony, Barbara and I visited the Cave of Mother Sea, soaking for long periods of time in her healing depths. When I emerged from the waters Barbara rubbed warm, soothing oils upon me. She prepared me special foods and broths. It was clear to me she was taking special care of me.

"Why do you fuss so?" I asked her one day as she rubbed oil upon my arm inside the damp cave.

"I am doing what any mentor does before the initiation of her apprentice," she said, pulling the oil down to the ends of my fingertips.

"That is untrue, Barbara," I said. "I have seen others initiated before me. They have not received half the care."

"I am only doing what I know I must do. It is not for you to question."

"But there is something you are not telling me."

"Do not ask me to tell you that which I cannot reveal," she said. She began to comb my hair, very gently separating the strands and combing it out toward her, then down along my back. I was looking out the opening of the cave. From inside one could only see the distant sea and the sky upon it. The light was bright, far away, casting beams through the cave's dusky interior. "I want to tell you something," Barbara said, stopping the movement of the comb. "You need to let me say it and not ask for explanations." She resumed combing. "Do you think you can do that?"

"I suppose," I said.

"You must know by now," she began, "that the task you are being asked to perform is not an easy one."

I turned my head to look at her. She turned it back to where it had been firmly with her hands. "What I want to say to you," she said into my right ear, her hands still holding my head firmly in place, the wet comb pushing against my right cheek, "is that I am here for you. Never start thinking that you are alone in this. I am here for you."

She put her arms around me and held me. I watched the space in front of me. A large white cloud crossed over the sun, eclipsing, for a moment, its light.

# CHAPTER 8

Beneath each temple is Her womb from which Her power rises up into the temple above it. Her womb is a crypt sunk down deep beneath the temple, centered around Her square pillar. Her power travels, from the depths of the earth beneath it, up through Her pillar, into the room above.

Frequently pilgrims are allowed to sleep within one of these wombs, awaiting sacred dreams or visions. Inside Her womb there is no light; no light may be brought in. Inside Her womb, only darkness.

Within this darkness I slept—floating, dreaming—the night before my initiation. I was relieved to be ending my long period of apprenticeship and intense seclusion, yet nervous about what would lie ahead in my role as a Snake priestess. What kinds of information would I process? Would I be strong enough to endure the cycle of bites?

Barbara had come to my room before she led me into the crypt. In her hands she carried two large, very long feathers, black with flecks of brown and stripes of white running through them.

"I never told you," she said, sitting down on the edge of my bed, "but before I became a Snake priestess, I was a bird explorer."

"Birds?" I said, sitting myself beside her.

"Yes, birds," she said, raising her shoulders and eyebrows simultaneously. "My relationship with birds began in my youth. At first it was simply an ability to coax them to eat out of my hands, but then they began to come to me spontaneously, landing suddenly upon my shoulder, perching confidently upon my fingers.

"They are such wonderful creatures," she continued, smiling softly. "So gentle and light. For a long time I thought I liked them even more than I liked people, but that has changed for me now.

"When I became a woman, I traveled the island exploring their nests and patterns of flight, identifying and recording their movements and cyclical journeying."

"Because of this you traveled so much," I said.

"Yes. That is right."

"Why did you not tell me of this before?"

"The information did not serve you any purpose, until now. You see, it was difficult for me to leave the birds for the call of the Snake for many reasons, but mostly because snakes do indeed eat birds. This I struggled with for a long time.

"It was my mentor who helped me to see that what one eats, one becomes. By ingesting bird, snake in fact becomes only another form of bird. Together with the shedding of her skin comes the release of feathers. Still today, I look for the bird within the snake. There are some things about ourselves that simply never leave us; however, we may alter them to make the way easier.

"These are two feathers of a snake eagle, a bird of magnificent power. She can hold a wriggling snake within her claws. She can swallow snake whole. It is my instinct that this is the medicine you will need to assist you in the path of full priestess. Tomorrow, you begin that journey. So it is that I present these to you, saying, 'Swallow her, Aureillia. Swallow her whole.'"

That night I slept with the feathers beneath me, thinking about Barbara, marveling on how even the birds adored her. I remembered the power of the feathers as I took them into my hands and the look of fierceness in her eyes as she surrendered them to me. I closed my eyes to that look and willed myself to sleep.

* * *

Within the pillar crypt I wait for the procession to begin. I wear the red and brown tiered skirt of initiation, the snakeskin apron around my waist, breasts exposed, a golden armband on either arm.

Barbara brings me the snake that has chosen me. I hold it before me, stretching it between my two hands. Its coarse skin rubs against my palms. This is the snake who will bite me, injecting me with a vision from which I shall transmute sacred knowledge. All priestesses are initiated within Her room which sits deep in the earth beneath the Center. In this room She is everpresent. It is here that She grants women the power to become priestess and bestows upon them Her magic. I have never been inside Her room. Only initiated priestesses are allowed. I know not the way. I have been told to follow the snake. From the door of the pillar crypt I extend the snake out in front of me, traveling down a dark, winding, weaving corridor. The walls tighten around me until they are almost pressing against me. The floor slopes downward. I am descending into the darkness, being squeezed into this space, the ceiling pressing down on my head. Behind me is Barbara followed by other initiated Snake priestesses.

"We have but one superior to whom we must answer," she had said to me, before she bid me farewell in the crypt. "It is She who presents us with our gifts. It is She who desires that you perform this work. It is She you must turn to when you need strength and assistance."

The corridor spills me into a small room filled with the familiar faces of the people I have missed. Sheena, Thela, Hypia, and Danelle stand watching as I walk through this entryway. They shall wait in this outer room as I pass through initiation, keeping silent watch as I receive the powers of a full priestess.

I want to stop and speak. I want to be with them, but I cannot. I must follow Barbara, who has passed into the room in front of me and is lighting small lamps set up close to the ceiling. The snake leads me to stand in the center of the room facing Her chair. It is a wooden chair, whose tall back blends into a mural of Her mountains behind it. Bench altars extend out on either side of it. It is hard to tell the chair from the painting, the painting from the wall whose picture leads me forward, traveling its terrain.

The room is small, with low ceilings. It feels as though it has been carved into the stone that encloses it.

The air vibrates and my body responds to a presence that can only be the Goddess. I bow in sacred gesture toward the chair that contains Her saying: "Only to be worthy."

The priestesses form a half-circle around me, leaving the throne and altar wall open. Barbara nods her head to me: it is time to begin. The priestesses sing a welcoming chant, each one bowing to me as I turn to them. Barbara leads me down a few steps into a deep, small, recessed area behind the large wall across from Her chair. I hand her the snake and coil myself into the tightest knot I can form. In the room above a drum begins a slow, steady rhythm. Barbara places the snake on the floor beside me. From the tight knot of the coil I stretch myself out along the floor, my breasts rubbing against the cool, smooth surface. The snake uncoils along with me, her unblinking eyes upon me, watching. She holds herself up slightly and her forked tongue emerges toward me. I slither up into another knotted coil, from there uncoiling slowly upward, dropping my snakeskin apron to the floor. I coil back down into a knot. I extend my arm out toward the snake; she swings herself toward me but strikes not. The drum beats louder, quickening. The vibration rises through me as I uncoil myself, raising my arms high into the air, dropping down again, being one with this sensuous movement, becoming this fluid dance, when I am alarmed out of it by a ferocious strike upon my right upper arm. A feeling of insult and hurt overwhelms me. Though fully aware that the bite is what I had wanted, the shock and insult from the stinging pain lingers within me.

Barbara grabs the snake and places it inside the pithoi beside us.

She takes my arm into her hands, firmly clasping a tight armband above the spot of the bite.

My vision blurs as I watch this, and as I look up at her face, she fades into darkness. I lose my physical body, toppling to the ground like so many tossed pebbles. She tries to stand me back up to walk me to my pillow where I shall receive my vision. I have no legs and fall instantly to the ground again. My body is being lifted and carried by many hands. Colors and flashes of bright lights invade my inner vision. Strong and bright, they bang their sharpened edges against the rounded contours of my inner skull, pushing mercilessly against the insides of my ears. I open my eyes. The temple spins above me so wildly that I shriek in fear.

A hand covers my eyes. "Do not open your eyes," Barbara's voice orders. I close my eyes and focus on the places where her hands meet my face. I can hear myself moaning, but the sound I am making is outside of myself. It does not seem to be a part of me. Then the moaning is overtaken by the noises I am hearing inside my head. A high pitched shrieking. There are still flashing lights but now I am concentrating on the noises, that shrieking. It is the most horrifying sound I have ever heard. A loud screech that ends abruptly. Cats. I recognize it finally as cats. Cats wailing.

I must be in distress because Barbara's hand grabs mine. "I'm here," her voice says. "Aureillia, stay with us." I feel her hand upon mine, grasping mine. I focus on that hand. That hand holds me to this earth. The shrieking becomes louder. There is something in my vision. It is smoke. Puffing clouds of billowing black smoke followed by a smell. An overwhelmingly putrid smell explodes through my senses, then it disappears.

# CHAPTER 9

When I woke up, my head throbbed and pounded so loudly within itself I thought I could not survive it. All that existed for me was the pain. I prayed for sleep until it at last overtook me.

The second time I woke up, the pain was less severe. I could hear but I could not open my eyes. I could not move my mouth to speak. I could not move any part of my body. I could feel. I could think. I could smell, but I could not move. I lay there trying to move, focusing on different parts of myself—an arm, a finger, an eyelid—telling it to move, begging it to move. I concentrated on it with every ounce of my energy, but I could not make anything happen.

I could hear Barbara and Danelle around me, fussing over me. Their talk, though tense and anxious about my condition, had a level of familiarity that surprised me. How long had I been asleep? I struggled to speak, to move my hand within Danelle's as he held it, to open my eyes as Barbara caressed my face, to do anything to let them know I was there with them, but I could not.

"It is not right that I let you stay here," Barbara said. "The other priestesses are becoming upset. There are no outsiders allowed in this temple."

"This is a special case. You know that. Tell them that," Danelle said. "I'm not leaving."

"I cannot reveal what I know."

"You have to me."

"Only because I care so about her—" Barbara's words stopped suddenly.

"What bothers you?"

There was a long pause. "I have done wrong," she said, "by telling you. It worries me, what I have done."

"You were right to tell me. She will only make it through this with both of us. But you must understand, now that I know, I will not leave her until she is well again."

I must have fallen back asleep then, for the next time I awoke I opened my eyes wide to see their two worried faces sitting on either side of me. Silk curtains hung around us, creating a small, private circle within the temple. An agreement had been made between

Barbara and the other priestesses that only within the curtains Danelle could stay with me, with Barbara escorting him in and out.

I did not tell them what I had heard. From the glances they passed between each other and the long silences at other times, I knew they were waiting for me to ask. But I did not. I did not want to know what I suspected.

After I was up and making progress in my recovery, the curtains were taken down. Danelle was no longer allowed inside the temple. Though I often saw him and Barbara talking outside the temple entrance, I pretended not to notice.

At the second bite I was taken less ill. As soon as the snake sank her long fangs into me, Barbara snatched my arm and sucked some of the venom into herself, spitting it out into a bowl beside her. I did not know she had planned on doing this and wanted to say something to stop her, but the venom already had me. The room spun around and strange noises filled my head. I could feel Barbara leading me away and sitting me down. The vision came swiftly.

Dust. Fire. Everywhere white dust. Such fine white dust, finer than the alabaster shavings that remain after a wall has been scrubbed smooth. So fine, so thick, so deep. It lies everywhere: on tall trees whose branches reach higher than our Center's peak. On the plants that spread growing through the fields, covering olive groves, on walkways, entire houses. The people walk through it. It is up to their knees in some places. Is this Crete? Our Crete? Yes: here is Knossos, here is the beach. It seems to fall from the air, this dust. It floats through the air. It fills the sea, a fine film upon the water. Plant life is dying under its oppressive weight. Fish emerge dying from Her waters. People sweep, frantically trying to clear it away.

I awoke the next day, only mildly ill. Barbara was sitting beside me.

"How did it go?" she whispered.

"Well," I said, sitting up. Pain rushed to my head. "I don't think I understand, though."

"You will, eventually."

"When?"

"The information is often passed to us in pieces. We shall use the same snake next time to see if she has more to tell you. When you think you have gotten a complete story, let me know."

"How will I know?"

"You will know. Like any story, it will have a beginning, a middle, and an end. The story is usually complete when you know which is which."

"When I know where it begins and where it ends?"

"That's right. When you feel you can tell it start to finish."

The white ash comes to me again in my next trance dance. Again, Barbara sucks some of the venom from my arm, and again I have a lesser reaction.

Food rots on plants under the weight of fallen ash. People of Minoa are thin and in want of food. High in the sky am I, hovering above a mountain inside which there has been a huge explosion of fire and gas. This is the source of the ash. It covers the skies, spreading itself far through the air, to the beaches of Crete. Below in the waters, huge waves thunderously pound onto the beaches of Knossos, forcing themselves high up into places that have never known the sea.

I wandered the beaches, full of worry. From what I had seen in my last vision, I knew what was to come next: earthquakes. Though there had not been any in my or my mother's lifetime, our oral myth was full of tales of the earth's thunderous rumblings—Her power swelling so fiercely within Her, She could not contain Herself—toppling the things we had built upon Her.

Whole Centers had toppled in upon themselves, creating years of rebuilding. By the time of my birth, the Center was on its third cycle of building.

I knew that I needed to pay close attention, to try to understand when it was these things were taking place. I feared I would not be able to.

Barbara had taken ill from the venom she took from me. "You know you have had more than your tolerable level," the herbalist said when she came to see her. "What are you trying to do?"

She did not know that I had heard this. When she came to me I could not help but notice how her thin knees were bent, barely holding her up.

"Aureillia," she confessed, "I have done a foolish thing. I must take some time to rest and regain strength. I must find a different way to reduce the venom in the bite for you." She leaned against the wall for support. "I shall pray for guidance. You will not dance again until I have received an answer."

"I shall stay and care for you."

"No. You shall go," she said, putting her hand upon my shoulder. Her face was thin and drawn. Dark circles surrounded her eyes.

"You shall go and refresh yourself. Go breathe the fresh air. Before you go, I must ask something of you."

"Yes, what is it?"

"I must ask for your forgiveness."

"Forgiveness?"

"I am your mentor. I have acted in an unthinking manner. Weakening myself to help you has done neither of us any good. I must remain strong to support you. I have been most careless. Please, forgive me."

"Because you ask my forgiveness, I grant it to you," I said, bowing before her, "though I do not believe there is anything to forgive. You must know that I am most deeply honored to be your apprentice."

# CHAPTER 10

Danelle was also no longer an apprentice. He had moved into a different workshop where he worked in solitude most of the time, specializing in miniature work. He had begun engraving intricate designs and patterns onto small, polished stones.

After Barbara had shooed me away, I went to look for him. I was surprised when his mentor told me he had moved into his own workshop across the hall. It was a large room for a single studio. Several tables were set up on the left side of the room with enlarging glasses propped in an upward position upon them. Danelle would eventually have to teach. These would be his student tables.

Danelle's own worktable was near the back wall, directly parallel to the doorway, which was on the right side of the room. It had several enlarging glasses upon it, each with a work in progress beneath. Tools were scattered upon it and several stools spread about it, in such a way that it appeared as though he moved between them frequently, working on many at once. Against the wall, beside the table, there were long shelves several rows high, which were packed with boxes and materials overflowing and tossed about as though someone had gone through them with great urgency.

It startled me to see the table and shelves in such a state of disarray, as Danelle was usually so meticulous and orderly. His room was tidy and neat—everything had its place. He carried with him the appearance of neatness—his hair cut short, face clean shaven, clothes hanging just right upon his body. This seemed not to be the case, however, in his work space.

Indeed, he, himself, even seemed disheveled when I found him: bending over a glass, lost in his work, his yellow shirt untucked and hanging over his shorts, his hair standing up in different places upon his head where he had brushed it back quickly with his hands.

It took him a while to notice me. I stood quietly observing him, wishing I could better see what it was his fingers were carving so carefully into that tiny stone beneath them, but his own head covered the enlarging glass as he looked through it. I began to explore what was beneath the other ones.

"Aureillia," he said, standing up suddenly. He shook his head so that his hair fell into place and pushed his shirt back into his shorts, making himself orderly again. It was clear from the dazed look in his eyes, however, that his mind was still in pieces.

"I'll come back later," I said, "Continue. Don't stop. I can see that I am interrupting."

"No, don't go. Please—give me a minute. I really do not want you to leave," he said.

"I will wait over there," I said, pointing to one of the student tables. "When you are ready you will show me, show me some of the things that you have been working on."

He nodded and sat back down to finish what I had shaken him from.

I sat on one of the small stools and waited. I was amazed to observe that Danelle had a window in his studio. Window studios were very rare. The window, in the middle of the inside wall, was at ground level with the outside. Though covered with bird netting, it offered a clear view up and out of the Center, following the dirt path up the hill which led to the Cave of Mother Sea. The most wonderful sounds filtered in through it: the fluttered tinklings of trees' leaves, bird chirpings, the distant murmur of intimate conversations, children playing.

"How did you ever manage it?" I asked, when he stood up and began rummaging through his shelves, "to get a window studio?"

"I seem to be very lucky," he said.

He carried a box over to the table where I sat—pulled a stool up close beside me so that our legs met—and began to take stone after stone out of the box. There were serpentine, obsidian, both white and black marble, and amethyst. Each one had a different engraving upon it. Some were so tiny, I could not imagine how he had accomplished it. Snakes, shells, butterflies, and trees, all possessing the same quality of incredible intricacy and flow of movement. It was as though he had captured a fleeting moment in time upon them—an indescribable feeling.

I could not stop looking at them, so captivating were they, continuously touching them, my fingers explored their curving lines of graceful dance.

"Danelle, these are magical," I remarked. "Why are they all tucked away in this little box?"

"I don't know what to do with them. I just keep carving them and carving them. It seems that this will be my specialty," he said, picking one up and rubbing his thumb over the engraving, "but I am sure I have not yet discovered what it is I shall do with them."

"Do with them? Give them all to me," I joked.

He brushed them over toward me in one long, dramatic, sweeping movement of his arm.

"What does your mentor say?" I asked.

"He says, 'Keep going where it leads you and there you shall be led.'"

"'There you shall be led'?" I repeated. "Yes, they do appear to be leading you somewhere—but where?"

"That I will know when I arrive there," he said, rubbing his eyes with his hands and smiling at me.

"You look tired," I said.

"The work is hard on my eyes."

"You must be careful," I said. "Perhaps you are working too hard."

He shrugged the question off. My eyes landed upon his hand, which was sitting on the table next to the stones it had carved: strong and long-fingered with well defined grace. I placed my hand upon it, tracing its precise contours and veins—confident knuckles—with my fingers.

"How would you feel about resting a bit and spending some time with me?"

"Perfect," he said, lifting my hand to his lips. "Just what I need." He pushed his stool back with one leg and stood up, pulling me up with him. We left the workshop together.

* * *

My feet could not lead me fast enough to Thela, whom I knew had brought forth a child from herself. At my initiation she had been large with life, but my illness had kept me from her.

As I walked into her room, I was greeted by the distinct smell of freshness. I found Thela seated upon the bed. The sweetest red lips enclosed her dark nipple, confidently, hungrily, extracting nourishing liquid. A small, perfect hand possessively held the smooth, rounded part of her breast.

Thela's long, black curls hung upon and over the child's tiny body, tiny shoulder blades, tiny rounded buttocks.

"Oh, Thela," I said, unable to remove my eyes from the mother and child.

Thela smiled, beaming pride at me. "It's quite something," she said, rubbing her hand over the thick black hair on her daughter's head.

She looked at my armbands, which I was required to wear at all times in public, then looked down at the bed.

"Look at you—full priestess now," she said.

"Yes, I managed it," I said. "There were times when I wondered whether I would."

"We are all very proud," she said, but it was there, the chasm, the gulf, the long and desolate canyon, that had grown between us in my absence.

"Forgive me, Thela; I am unable to discuss it now. I would like very much to tell you everything, if I could," I said, trying to stop it, to stretch myself across the gap and keep it from growing any wider. But the futility of my efforts was obvious even as I sat there.

"It's all right, Aureillia," Thela said, patting her daughter—over Thela's shoulder now—until she released a loud bubble of air. "I feel it too. But it is only temporary. We will find each other again."

I nodded my head.

Thela handed the child to me. "Leida," she said, "meet your Aunt Aureillia, the Snake priestess."

I took the child into my arms. A look of satisfaction covered her little wizened face. Her arms stretched out toward me as her eyes curiously explored me.

"Hello, Leida," I said, pulling her near my face and taking in her newness. She giggled happily within my embrace. "Oh," I said, engaging her eyes, "I have a feeling we are going to be great friends."

* * *

Danelle and I walked along the beach. The sun was high in the sky above us. I was silent, thinking first about Barbara, then about my visions.

I wanted to tell Danelle but I knew I could not. Snake priestesses were allowed to divulge the information they received only to their mentor or in sanctioned ritual. I was not even finished with this snake; not sure of the whole story.

Nor did I want Danelle to know the truth about how ill Barbara had become as he would know that the same fate might be awaiting me. I could tell from the way he looked at me that he was already concerned enough.

I stopped walking and leaned against a soft wall of sand carved into the hill behind me. I looked out at the waters and sighed.

"Is it very painful?" Danelle said, holding my arm within his two hands, his thumbs rubbing the purple two dot marking of my last bite.

"In every way possible," I said, closing my eyes to the feel of his open mouth upon it—his tongue exploring it, moving up my arm, under and through the rings of my armband.

"I worry so about you," he said, moving himself close to me so that I could feel the heat of his body beneath the soft fabric of his shirt. I looked into his face, so close to mine, noticing for the first time tiny, scratchy lines around his eyes. His hair, soft and feathery, filled my hands.

How was he able to be so big and open—so present? I was overcome with feeling. Pools of emotion surfaced within my eyes.

He took me to him and with his magic mouth kissed either of my eyes, following their streams of water with his soft lips before settling upon my mouth. I pulled him to me, passionately loving him, until he surrendered himself to me on the soft sands beneath us.

* * *

Barbara had been instructed to squeeze the venom out of me, pinching the area of the bite with her fingers into a bowl of warm water. She had also been told to make herself stronger by walking a good portion of the day, her legs being entirely too weak. I joined her in her long daily walks, finding it more difficult to keep up with her as time passed. My legs became thick and strong. I was pleased.

Barbara decided that the long walks were an opportunity for her to do some bird exploring. We began directing our walks around bird haunts, sometimes sitting on a craggy cliff for hours, waiting.

Other times, she would stop walking suddenly and point up into a tree, saying, "Look, there—a nest."

After a long time looking I would at last see it, there in the tree's long and stretching branches, a small brown and gray collection of twigs.

We had been watching a particular nest of golden oriole eggs suspended from a fork in an evergreen, ready to burst forth with life at any moment.

One day, as we approached the nest hopefully, quietly, we were stopped suddenly by the sight of a newly hatched chick lying lifeless on the ground beneath it.

When Barbara saw this, she collapsed to the ground, releasing deep, uncontrolled sobs. She knelt beside the bird, its tiny body broken from the fall, and covered her face with her hands and rocked back and forth.

I knelt down beside her and put my arm around her back, as I had never seen it—curved and vulnerable.

"I know. I know," she said. "It is only a bird. I know, it's just another one of Her mysteries that we have to accept. But why?

Why?" she moaned, her voice swelling with anger. "Why must the little ones suffer?" She was looking at me but not seeing me. Her face was that of a child's, full of question and frustration, puffy and blotched red. "I try," she said, "but I can't understand. I just don't understand."

This snake has much more to tell me. She bites me harshly on the inside of my wrist. Blood gushes. Barbara sinks the wound into warm water while squeezing and pinching, intensifying the pain. I am weak. I am falling forward. I am already seeing it.

While she is still squeezing the blood out, blood is splashing my vision. "No. No," I hear myself saying.

"Stop moving. Stop moving, Aureillia," Barbara's voice is pleading.

But I must crawl away. I must go somewhere, anywhere. Axes slam themselves hard into the bare flesh of shoulders and arms and bare backs as they flee. A priestess is injured. She is crawling away but he follows her. She stands up. She looks at him, meeting his eyes with fierceness in hers before he stabs his sword into her womb.

"No. No. Stop. No." I cannot stop moving. My body. It jerks and kicks. I must get out of here.

Barbara is holding me down. "Please. Help," I hear her saying. "Someone, help."

They are holding me down. There are many of them. I know not who they are. I cannot see. I thrust and thrust until I cannot thrust any more. My breathing is heavy. I give in. My forehead is wiped with a cool cloth. This feels good. I try to smile at this but I don't know if I am smiling. I want to say something, but I cannot speak. I am looking upon the port. The port of Knossos. There are foreign ships in the marina. I have seen their banners before. They are from the large land to the north. It is from these ships that these brutal men have come. They run through the streets, which still bear the traces of white ash. Something is different. Buildings have collapsed in on themselves: their stones and rocks stand in the streets and pathways. There have been earthquakes. Our island is devastated. Our beautiful buildings falling around themselves in rubble—blood flowing within the debris.

I was sick. I was so very sick, but more than sick, I was sad; saddened to the very core. I love this island, Minoa, so very much. I could never have imagined the things I had seen. The tears rolled endlessly from my eyes, sliding down my cheeks as I lay in recovery. Barbara wiped them away patiently. "So sad. So sad," she said, dabbing my cheeks dry with a soft cloth. "So very sad."

Danelle came to sit with me, but he was clearly distracted. He would enter the curtains suddenly, having walked through the temple unannounced, upsetting the the other priestesses.

"Danelle, you must tell me when you are to come, so that I may arrange it with the other priestesses," Barbara repeated.

"I am sorry," he would say in an uncharacteristically uncaring way, "I keep forgetting to arrange it with you, and then I just need to see her."

His behavior concerned me, but I could do nothing about it. I could not move anything but my eyes. One day, after sitting beside me quietly for a while, he began shifting in his chair. "Please, Aureillia," he pleaded, "I know you can hear me." He stood up and began to pace around within the curtained-off area.

"I'm going to tell you whether you can or not," he said, dropping himself back heavily into the chair beside me and taking my hand. "You see," he began, "the stones I was carving, they kept stacking up and stacking up into piles and piles until, finally, they began to bother me. I spread them out upon a long bench outside my studio and put a note above them letting people know they could take them. You would not have believed it. They were gone in one day. First, it was only a few people passing by who stopped and took some but, as the day progressed, it became clear that others were coming into the Center with the sole intention of obtaining one. It was very exciting, watching people look through them and choose one that was right for them. I was quite satisfied and decided, 'That's it. I shall make them and place them here for whoever wants them.'"

"At least, that is what I thought I had decided. I could not seem to stop making them, and I did not want them to continue to stack up in such a way. It seemed the perfect solution, until the other day.

"As I was working, a man entered my studio timidly. "'Excuse me,' he said. 'Forgive me for interrupting. Please—I was wondering if you could make one of these amulets for my daughter.'

"'Amulets?' I said

"'Yes, well, that's what they are, aren't they?' he queried. 'That's what everyone is calling them.'

"'Amulets?'

I repeated. I was shocked to hear them referred to in such a way.

"'I am sorry. Whatever they are. My daughter saw one and liked it. I thought how nice it would be to have one made just for her.'

"'I would have to meet her,' I answered.

"He brought her to me and we spent some time together in my studio. After she left, I sat down and carved a design into the stone from the impression she had left upon me. It was an interesting thing to do, and I did enjoy it, but now they are coming to me, more and more each day, all requesting special stones designed just for them and I—" He stopped and turned suddenly. Barbara was standing behind him.

"Go on," she said.

His face reddened. He said nothing, only looked down at the blankets upon me, rubbing my hand within his.

She came to sit on the other side of me. "I know you wish to speak to Aureillia," she said, "but she is not at the moment available. If you need someone to talk to, I am willing to stand in. I do not think that she would mind."

He remained silent, still not looking at her.

"Are you really so private, or is there something else?" Barbara asked.

He nodded his head, indicating yes.

"It is not I who have chosen her to do this," she said.

He released a heavy sigh and dropped his head into his hands.

"It will serve Aureillia no purpose if—" He raised his hand to stop her words. "You are right. I am sorry. I have been unfair."

There was a long stretch of silence. At last Danelle sat back in his chair, crossed his arms in front of himself, and looked at Barbara.

"What is it about this new development in your work that disturbs you so?" Barbara asked.

"I am not sure if this is what I want to do—to design stones for people as they come to me."

"You could try. Try it and if it is not for you, you shall know," she said. "But you must follow these leads. Though they take you other than where you expect, they are the only markers along the way."

He nodded his head in agreement to this.

"It is not so different," she said, "the work we do from yours. I can tell you now that it is about more than listening. It is about being able to hear."

He looked at her with such reverence that she flushed slightly, shifting her gaze to the floor. He persisted, continuing to look at her for a long while until she returned her gaze to him. They sat looking at one another until he let himself say it. "I deeply resent this," he said.

"As do I," Barbara said. "As do I."

* * *

When I was well again, Barbara and I resumed our walks, my legs needing it as much as hers. After many days of brisk walks in silence, I said, "I think I have completed a cycle. I think I have a prophecy to report."

"Do you?" Barbara turned to me in surprise, her face flushed from walking. Sweat stood upon her forehead. She had regained her strength and looked remarkably healthy. She put her hands upon her hips and looked at me. I loved her so intensely. Each time we parted, parts of myself tugged urgings after her. Every morning she was there, ever so cheerful, smiling at me. Her perfectly straight teeth shining between purple lips, forcing me into the day just from want to be with her.

"Yes," I said shakily, suddenly nervous, "I do not understand how to do this. I would like to tell you."

"Yes. Do," she said, eagery. "Tell me."

"I don't know."

"Come, you can do it."

I had rehearsed this in my mind many times in the past few days. We stood on a wide, stretching beach. I turned to face the water. Light brown sands and open air spread everywhere around us, yet I felt I had not enough room.

"It's all right, Aureillia. Let it be what it is." I squeezed my eyes shut. "A volcano erupts on an island to the north of us," I began. "Our island becomes covered in an ashy substance. We suffer greatly due to loss of food. Soon, earthquakes come, then Crete is devastated from one disaster after another. Our people are weak and vulnerable." I stopped and inhaled deeply.

"That was fine," Barbara said.

But I stopped her. "I'm not finished," I said, putting my face into my hands. "I am afraid to say the next part," I trembled, looking up at her. "As though saying it might make it come true. I'm not sure I have all the information correct."

"Just tell me what you saw," Barbara encouraged, standing closer to me, almost leaning over me. "Close your eyes and tell me what you saw as you saw it."

I sat down and wrapped my arms tightly around my knees. Barbara sat beside me, facing me. I closed my eyes and listened to the sound of the waves. The breeze blew my hair. I breathed in again. "There are ships," I said. "I recognize their banners. They are from the large land to the north. We know these people. They come off their ships and with their swords and knives of bronze, with the most sacred labrys we have fashioned with our own hands, they murder us, plundering all, until they have overtaken our island."

"When?" Barbara asked urgently, moving even closer to me.

"I don't know. It is not now. Things are different, but not terribly different. It does not seem that the day is so far away."

"You have done well, Aureillia," she said. She crossed her arms upon her raised knees and looked out toward the waters. Her white skirt tossed wildly in the wind.

"The council of elders will need to hear this," she said, digging her heels into the sand. "I must get you into the next Snake Goddess festival. We must prepare for oral prophecy."

Barbara was so serious at that moment. All the relief I had experienced from having completed a cycle escaped me, quickly turning into dread. "So soon?"

"The council of elders desires to hear information of this sort immediately. We are required to report it."

"I am not ready for oral prophecy." I felt cold. The wind blew, raising bumps upon my skin.

"I will help you. I must go," she said. She stood up and brushed the sand off her dress before leaving me. Halfway down the beach she stopped, turned around and came all the way back to me. "Aureillia, I am so sorry. Your first completed cycle!" She put her arms around me and warmly embraced me. "I am so very proud! You have done extremely well."

She turned and left me again. I stood and watched her disappear.

CHAPTER 11

I had to borrow a robe, the festival arrived so quickly. Barbara and I had been working steadily, first composing, then repeating—over and over—my prophecy.

Snake priestess festivals occurred four times per annum, at the dark time of the moon, and were always well attended. The people of Minoa were very interested in what She had to say. They wanted to hear it directly from us, rather than wait for it to become part of the oral myth. They wanted to decide for themselves the meaning in the messages.

For days after a Snake priestess festival the streets would be alive with chatter. Stories were repeated, interpretations given, arguments raised over the proper analysis of verses sung.

It was always interesting to hear the way prophecies returned to us. Often the meanings were distorted, but sometimes ideas were pointed out that had not been previously noticed. The temple of the Snake Goddess became alive with chatter as well.

Her prophecies were spoken in the smaller west court, from within the giant, carved wooden image of a Snake Goddess. As a child, I had been fascinated by this moving wooden speaker, her eyes hollow and deep. Large wooden arms entwined with snakes reached out toward the crowd in pleading gesture. Each hand carried a lamp, the only light within this wide, triangular, open-air court.

At the festivals, after the prophecies had been spoken, certain priestesses made themselves available for direct consultation. Smaller wooden statues were erected in the back of the hall, from behind which the priestesses would answer questions of a personal nature for festival participants.

Lines of people are already forming as we walk in long procession from the temple of the Snake Goddess into the west court at nightfall. Each of us who will speak carries with her a light.

The robe hangs loosely around me in flowing black folds. I sit in my seat and await my turn. From within Her statue, which is rolled around the court, other priestesses speak concerning matters of trade and weather. One tells the story of a swan; a swan who became a woman or a woman who became a swan. I am unable to focus on the words, the lines of my own verse tumbling over and over inside my head.

Her wooden statue is rolled over to me by Barbara and another Snake priestess. The statue is three times larger than I. I climb the ladder within her until my face reaches the opening that is her mouth, with a large triton shell placed within it to amplify my voice.

Within Her, I am rolled around this court, my voice echoes out over the scratching sound of dirt caught between Her wheels and the floor below them. Speaking I say:

> "From Arcadia they will come to destroy us
> After a fine, white, all-consuming ash
> Falls from the skies everywhere above us
> Covering, suffocating plants and grass
> After giant waves crash over our beaches
> The force of Her water pounding far away reaches
> When we have been devastated by earthquakes
> And have not food ourselves to take
> As our buildings lie in rubble around us
> Those who now covet our most sacred labrys
> Shall come in bands and hoards
> And with their knives and swinging swords
> Take Knossos—alas, our entire island
> Minoan blood staining their hands."

The great court stands in silence as I descend the stairs within her and walk back to my seat. Each of my movements can be heard, even the rustling of the fine silk fabric of my robe breaking sharply, painfully, through the stillness like scattering shells.

Later, I found Danelle at our meeting place. I sat down next to him, landing heavily with a sigh.

"How did it feel," he asked, "to speak in front of others in such a way?"

"Let's not speak of it, Danelle. Please," I said, dropping my head between my knees.

He lifted it with his hands so that I was looking at him. "Aureillia, today was your first oral prophecy. Do not deny its importance."

"Your work is so beautiful," I said, "so pure and inspired. You are so full of magic. Why do you bother with me?"

"Bother with you?" he said, pulling my head to his chest. "You are the bravest person I know."

"Brave?"

"Do not underestimate your strength, Aureillia. I know I never do." His hand was in my hair, his fingers pulling at it gently, tickling me with pleasure.

I collapsed into him, pulling his arms around me. "Do you know what they said to me," he asked, "when you were through? The ones who know that we share one another?"

I closed my eyes and shook my head to better feel his fingers within my hair. "No."

"They said to me," he said, "'only the strongest ones get chosen for jobs such as these! And I nodded my head to them. I said, 'I know.'"

# CHAPTER 12

The council of elders requested a private meeting with me. In their council room, on the upper floor of the Center building, we sat in circle day after day. They listened as I closed my eyes and described to them everything I had seen throughout the whole cycle of visions.

They recorded while I spoke, asking me to slow down or repeat, interrupting with frequent questions, after which they would review their notes, and question me again.

For days we worked, meticulously recording my detailed descriptions of every piece of every building, each plant and person, every part and location of the island as I had seen it.

From these descriptions, they and those who would come after them could determine when the time of these occurrences was drawing near. From the buildings I described that were not yet in existence, especially, could they gauge their predictions. These, we spent the most time on—any new building—examining carefully the structures around it, watching closely for any alterations; attaining precise locations.

All knew the events I foretold could not be altered yet perhaps, through warning, certain things could be avoided.

Before the last earthquake, which was prior to my mother's or my lifetime, the community of Knossos had broken apart.

As in my vision, a volcano on a nearby island forewarned the residents of Crete of an earthquake's arrival. There were those in the community who began to argue that the Goddess was angry, demanding life. "If we give to her, she will not take," they blasted at the community meeting.

"She will take no matter what," people in opposition argued. "Giving up life will not prevent an earthquake from happening."

Sacrificial practices had been going on for some time in many of the lands surrounding Crete. "Look how they prosper," they argued back, "through these practices. Look at how wealthy they are. Indeed it must satisfy the Goddess if she rewards them so."

"It is not because of their practices that they are wealthy, but because of their overuse of aggression and unfair policies. It is this which brings them their wealth, and to far too few."

These arguments continued for days. No decision was reached. The community was full of anger and resentment, remaining divided in opposing factions.

But in the end, a day and place were selected. In a mountain sanctuary, just northwest of Knossos, half of the community assembled. After certain, agreed-upon rituals were performed by the group as a whole, a high priest, high priestess, and a newly initiated boy entered the temple. With a long, sharp sword, the priestess sliced that young man's throat, taking his life.

As they began collecting the blood flowing out of him to offer to the Goddess, She trembled. With ferocity, She rumbled and shook. The shrine toppled in upon them, killing all inside as well as many of the worshippers outside.

The story has become a part of our oral myth. We are all taught it. It lives within each of us, hauntingly, and is referred to again and again by those concerned with preserving the ideas and beliefs of Minoa.

To this day, no one goes near the place of the incident. It lies desolate, isolated. As Minoans, we are united again in our belief that human sacrifice is never the answer.

This private inquiry was one of the various ways the council of elders had devised to try to deal with issues such as these. Through the answers I gave, we came to realize that these events would not happen in my lifetime, but soon thereafter.

It was exhausting work, but I pushed through it, repeating myself over and over, knowing that if any good could come of this prophecy, it would be through this very communication. Though the information I had shared was unpleasant, when we finished, and each one approached me, thanked me individually and told me how helpful I had been, I felt a feeling of accomplishment I had not achieved through oral prophecy.

# CHAPTER 13

Most priestesses would have moved on by now, moved away from their mentor, into their occupation. Barbara had said nothing to me about this. I dared not ask. I did not expect to be going on to my fifth trance dance with her, but I could not imagine going without her. We did not speak of it. The unspoken words hung between us. We approached the rounded moon in silence.

The snake caught us both unaware, striking me fiercely on the ankle. Barbara tried desperately to squeeze some venom out, yet, due to the location of the bite, she was unable to. I vomited and fell to the floor.

I am immediately transported back to the place I visited in my initiation. A place of smoke and fire and screaming cats. This time I am able to see as well as hear. I see women. They are tied to poles. They are being burned alive. The putrid smell. It was the smell of burning flesh. This is no accident. These women are being burned for a reason. There are a lot of them. This is happening in a public way. There are a lot of people watching. Standing there, watching. Doing nothing. Some of the bound women scream as the fire eats their bodies away. Some do nothing. The fire consumes them. It is lit and controlled by men in black robes who chant around them as though this is some sort of ritual celebration. The wood beneath the women is constructed in an intricate design. Much thought went into how this fire would burn. I see them. The cats. They scream as they are thrown to their death by these men in black robes. They stand there and throw cats into the roaring fire with the women. The cats catch fire instantly.

Their screams are so full of pain and horror that it hurts the ears. Some people huddle together in fear.

This is the only emotion I see. The people are dressed so darkly. There is no joy here. I can hear myself screaming, muffled and distant.

"Do something. Somebody. Somebody do something. Someone help these poor women!"

* * *

When I woke up I was a tangled mass in the corner of the temple. There were blankets wrapped around me. Sage burned heavily above me. Barbara sat preparing a tonic beside me.

"You're back," she said when she saw my eyes open.

That look was in her eyes again, one of concerned compassion. Only now did I know why it was there. "You were screaming. You were making horrible noises. We had to close the doors to the temple."

My head hurt with such ferocity that I could not lift it off the floor. "Tell me about the place where I am now, Barbara," I said. "Tell me about the beginning."

"The earth was born of the egg of the Serpent," she said, kneeling close to me, taking my hand into hers and gently caressing it. "After the egg had formed within Her, She released it into the sky. The egg split open, releasing many more eggs, among them earth, moon, and sun. Snake roamed upon the earth, shedding Her skin. From Her skin, people were formed. Since we are of Snakeskin, Snake has much wisdom to offer us, one bite at a time. Snake is all knowing. She planted trees. She filled the seas. She gave the earth beauty. She is our mother, always beckoning us back into Her egg, into the dark mysteries that are life."

I could hear snakes hissing in the pit below us. A wave of nausea washed over me. "Why, Barbara?" I said finally to her.

"Not all prophecies are good," she answered quickly.

"Will any of mine be good?"

She sat there looking at the wall in front of her, rubbing her hand over mine repeatedly, more to calm herself than me. I could see her swallowing hard and knew she was fighting back tears.

"For years I heard tell of you," Barbara whispered. "The prophetess of darkness; a woman of great strength and courage. I lived in awe of this woman until it came to me in a vision that it was I who would mentor you. Then my heart grew heavy and I feared you. 'I don't want the job,' I screamed to no one. I looked upon Her sculpture with anger and resentment." She took a deep breath and moved her legs into a crossed position beneath her, arranging the silk of her sleeveless purple dress upon her legs. "The first time I met you," she said, looking at me, "my insides cried for you, your youth, your hope. But I have come to understand that I have no choice. In this, I have no choice."

"I do," I said. I was full of anger. "I will leave here. I will not return here, and then both our pain will be ended."

"It is unwise to try to avoid purpose," Barbara said.

For two days I could not walk. Barbara gathered some other priestesses to help move me to a cave with an opening to the sea.

"Our most healing ally is water," she said. "You must look upon the sea. You must feel the sunlight." For days I lay inside the cave listening to the rhythm of the waves, the never-ending pulse of their song. From where I lay I could see a framed picture of the world outside. Birds flew by. The sun rose and set. The moon danced upon the water. I lay on my side, cuddled beneath deep blankets, watching.

Barbara brought me broths of mushrooms and burdock root, teas of mint and marjoram, and tonics for strengthening. She tried to drag me out into the sunlight when it shone itself strongly in the sky, but I protested so loudly that she stopped. I spoke no words; I listened ever so carefully to the birds. One night in a dream I saw Danelle searching for me. I asked Barbara to bring him to me.

He came the next day and stayed with me, only leaving me to sit outside in the afternoon sun. Even then, he remained within sight. His patient back became another part of the picture that I watched. After a few days and much coaxing, I let him drag me out to sit with him there. I lay beside him with my head upon his folded knees, my body soaking in the sun like a thirsty sponge.

When I was well enough to walk, he helped me back to his room. "Please, tell me what it is," he asked me for the first time after tucking me into his bed, but no words would come to me.

Barbara came to me the next day. With frantic gestures I sent her away.

Still, she came every day. I could feel her presence outside the room. I could hear her and Danelle discussing me.

One day I awoke up to a smell that I liked: jasmias. It was the first time in a long time that I was aware of the world around me. That night, when Danelle returned from the Center, he found me out of bed and sitting up, bathed and dressed. A vase full of jasmias sat proudly upon his table.

His face was hopeful when he entered the room and saw me. "How are you?" he asked, scooping me up into his arms. But that's all there was. Still, no words came to me.

I took a job picking berries. Every day I walked down the dirt road from Danelle's room to the berry patch and picked berries until my hands bled.

"Do not work so hard and so long," they would say to me in the evenings when I turned my berry pick in, looking at my hands in disgust. Only then would I realize that I was bleeding. Even then, I could not feel the pain.

Every morning I would sling my deep berry basket over my shoulder and walk down the small dirt pathway, overgrown with trees, that led from Danelle's block to the main road. As I unlatched the gate between the entrance to his block and the road, I would see Barbara standing on the other side of the road, waiting. I would not speak to her. I would keep walking. She would follow me the whole way. She would wait outside the berry patch. When I was finished working, she would follow me back. She would stand outside Danelle's room until he returned from the Center at which time they would visit for a moment before she left.

Danelle would come into the room and immediately wash my hands in a bath of thyme and marjoram, then wrap them tightly in bandages. "There is no need to punish yourself this way," he would mutter, kissing the backs of my hands.

Some days I could feel his frustration when he walked in and again found me there, helpless as a child, my hands cut and bloodied. I could sense that he wanted to scream at me, yell some sense into me, scold me. I would have liked to do the same to myself. I would not have taken offense had he done so, but he never did. He would look at me, his eyes sparking with anger, then inhale deeply and turn it into compassion. I would return him a look of gratitude.

In the evenings we would lie under the stars at our meeting place up on the hill overlooking the sea. He would tell me stories, some that he had heard, some that he had experienced, or talk of his work. I would lie with my head upon his chest, listening. The sound of his voice echoing inside him brought me great comfort. I never wanted him to stop talking.

He would bring me small figurines or seal stones he had sculpted. I held each one inside a leather pouch I wore hanging down from the belt around my waist. Before going to sleep he would unbandage my hands and wash them again, letting them heal in the cool night air.

He always left early in the morning to comb the beaches for things to sculpt on or with. He tried to get me to go with him, but I never did.

One day it was exceptionally warm. There were very few berries left. I finished my work early and followed the dirt path in the other direction—toward the shore. Barbara followed me. The water was so very blue and calm, beckoning. I could not resist its call. I felt almost pulled and tugged by it. I took my clothes off and went in for a swim. How deliciously soothing the water was. It stung my scratched hands. I welcomed the feeling. Any feeling was a relief. Now they could begin to heal.

Under the water I swam and floated. When I came up for air, I could see Barbara sitting far up on the left hand corner of the beach, watching.

After a while I met a dolphin. It seemed to have appeared out of nowhere. It was highly unusual to see one so alone as this one. I wondered if it was sick. It seemed sad and languid. I tried to engage it in play or get it to take me for a ride, but it would not.

"What is it?" I asked, caressing its back gently. It swam around me for a while slowly, rubbing up against me halfheartedly, floating slowly beside me on its side. Then I heard a voice. The voice again. The voice which speaks to me. The voice of the serpent, yet clearly coming from the dolphin.

"I don't want to be a dolphin," it said.

"Silly creature," I chuckled, "a dolphin is what you are. How could you be anything but what you are?"

As the words came out of my mouth, I stopped laughing.

"Who are you?" I said angrily.

"You know who I am," the voice said, bouncing over the surface of the water.

I turned around. The beach was empty, even the left corner. "Barbara!" I screamed to nothing. "Barbara!" I screamed again, slapping the water with my right hand. The dolphin jumped in the distance before swimming away.

I began to laugh, a laugh I had not laughed in many moons. A laugh of breadth and expansion; a laugh breaking open my closed insides, offering relief. The wind echoed my laugh back at me. The water vibrated it up through my body. I laughed until I could not laugh any more. I looked around at the beauty that surrounded me. I breathed it in.

When I got out of the water, the berries I had left in my basket had turned into lilies. I took their huge, pure white flowers to my face, accepting their essence, and rubbed their dripping moisture upon it. When I walked back to the temple, I carried them with me.

Barbara's straight back was sitting upon her pillow. I approached her from behind.

"If a person wants to avoid visions," she said, while I was still behind her, "they do not enter Mother Sea alone."

I knelt down before her, bowing my head. "Please, forgive me," I said, taking her hand into mine.

"There is nothing to forgive," she said, squeezing my hand with such intensity that it hurt. "Nothing to forgive."

# CHAPTER 14

For one full lunar cycle Barbara and I worked together preparing me to better handle the information which was to be given to me. There were no more secrets and silences. Now that I knew the nature of my prophecies, we would work together on ways to assist me in receiving them. Barbara would remain my mentor until the snakes were finished with me. I was relieved at that. I never wanted her to leave me.

We did many exercises to strengthen my physical body. I spent much time sitting silent time with Barbara guiding me in exercises of detachment. In these exercises we constructed a protective shell in my mind: a large egg twice the size of my body, inside which I would sit. The inside of the egg was my own space. I painted the walls light blue. I even brought actual blankets my mother had woven me into it as well as pendants Danelle had sculpted for me.

We worked on that egg until it got to the point that all Barbara had to say was "You are inside your egg," and I was there. Then we created a peep-hole through which I would watch the visions and collect the information that was given to me while sitting safely inside my egg. In no way was I to become involved in what I was seeing. The shell was the barrier between me and the visions; the peep-hole my window.

We began to work in a small room toward the back of the temple so as not to disturb the other priestesses. There we practiced, me seeing again what I had seen last time through the peep-hole of my egg. Three times during the exercise, I was given something to eat, as I would be given food three times during trance. The food would keep my body in the present, to remind me that what I was witnessing was not happening to me.

I had become committed to my role as a priestess of the Snake Goddess. I understood that this task needed to be done. It was to be done by me with Barbara as my guide. I no longer questioned anything she said. I listened and obeyed. It was to the Snake Goddess that I turned for strength, praying to Her constantly. It was through Her that I realized that this job had a beginning, a middle, and an end. The sooner I got on with it, the sooner it would end. This skin too, I would shed.

The night before my trance dance, I meditated beneath the sculpture of the Snake Goddess. The sun set behind Her, casting the shadow of Her upon me; Her brave, strong, upraised arms encircled me.

"Owl, dolphin, and snake will help you." She said, "Seek the wisdom in their medicine."

I dance the dance of the snake. I coil and uncoil my body. I slither. I crawl. I extend my arm to her for the magic bite that speaks; it snaps my arm like the sting of a swinging rope. Barbara snatches my arm, submerging it instantly in a vessel of water. After squeezing quite a bit of the venom out, she places an extracting poultice upon it, then clasps the armband efficiently over that.

I am able to walk to my pillow, and am still conscious when she hands me the first piece of flatbread. I get inside my egg. My blankets lie upon its floor, my precious pendants scattered upon them. I take the miniature sculpture of the Snake Goddess that Danelle carved for me so long ago and hold it to my chest within my right hand. I hear sounds. I know where I am going, back to the place I left so many moons ago. I slowly open my peep-hole. Yes, here I am. Back in the place of horrors. The fires are not yet lit. The wood stands waiting. The poles are erected, but the action takes place to the side where a woman sits, unclothed, hands tied behind her back, surrounded by several men dressed in heavy black clothing. One asks her questions. She answers. He asks again. Again she answers.

Already there is a difference in the fact that this time, I am not there but only a spectator looking through a window at events being shown to me. What strikes me immediately is that the people who are actually there, crowded in a circle around them, act as though they too are looking through a peep-hole.

The man who does the questioning wears a large pendant of two crossed lines around his neck. It hangs down strongly within the thick material of his shirt, its gold reflecting what little sun comes through the clouded sky above them. In his hands there is a large book that he keeps referring to. He lifts his arms in huge gestures and movements as he walks and speaks around her. His presence is overwhelmingly large and threatening. Behind the crowd there is a cart upon which other women sit. They too are unclothed. Around their mouths are tied scarves so they may not speak, and their hands and legs are connected with black rings. Many of them appear to be very ill. Some have many bruises.

Suddenly a hand reaches inside my egg. Frightened, I almost scream until I realize it is Barbara, handing me more food. Another piece of flatbread, several slices of quince. I want to refuse it, but then I remember our agreement.

The timing turned out well, as after what I was to see next, I surely would not have eaten.

The woman sits in the chair. Although the man is the one in control, he seems to have fear of her. It is very strange, since she is the one bound and naked before him, yet he struts around her almost tauntingly, clearly afraid of touching her except to hurt her. He asks the question again. Again she answers. I know not the language in which they speak, but I do recognize that she has given him the same answer to the same question so many times that it is tiresome. Now he consults with the other men, who are now all seated on the same side of a table watching him. They shake their heads in agreement to what he says. He approaches another table, which has a variety of strange looking instruments upon it. He takes one into his hand and carries it over to the woman. She looks at it with recognition, yet remains calm. He takes her hand into his in a seemingly tender gesture. He inserts her thumb into the space between two iron bars, which he screws together until her thumb is pressed tightly, smashed between the two bars. He asks her the question again. She looks directly into his eyes. She repeats the same answer. He tightens the bar in angry ferocious movements until blood from what used to be her thumb drips down to her knees, streaming down the length of her bare legs. I look away, up to the ceiling of my egg with its blue softness. I squeeze the Snake Goddess between my two hands, breathing deeply. I return to the window. Sweat beads up furiously upon her forehead. He again repeats the question. She returns her answer. He jerks a thin, black rope from around his waist and lashes her with it several times across her face. He returns to the table of men; they talk again, nodding all in agreement. He returns to her. The defiance on her face has been broken a bit by the unexpected whips to the face. Her eyes water from the sting. He removes the contraption from her thumb and returns it to the table from which it came.

He picks up a long tube. He again approaches her, holding up the tube for her to see. He asks her the question. She answers her answer. He inserts the tube into her mouth, pushing it down her throat. She must not be able to breath, her body wriggles and writhes. He yells something loudly. A young boy runs to him with a bail full of water. Together they pour the water into the tube. The women in the cart moan and look away. Some shed tears. The crowd watches; some eagerly. Some call out words to the woman. Some whisper among themselves. None, however, protest what is happening to this woman. What could she possibly have done. I am struck by the realization that before they were burned, those other women must also have endured this same treatment. Anger wells up within me.

Water is poured and poured into the tube, going directly into and down the throat of this poor woman, who at first contorts and struggles until she loses strength and collapses. The tube is removed. She vomits up the water in several vile vomiting sessions until there is no more. Still her body moves in the act of vomiting. She lies on the ground in front of these people, her arms still tied behind her back. No one goes to her. The man again approaches her. He asks her his question. She answers a different answer. It is the answer he wanted. He smiles and kicks her broken body. Then he shouts something. Two men also dressed in heavy black clothing carry her away. She is taken inside a very dark room, where iron rings are placed around her hands and feet. She is left there in the dark. Alone where no one can see or hear her, she releases sobs of desperation and anger. Finally, the tears he had wanted. The ones she did not give him.

*   *   *

"It is owl's vision that most often astounds us," Barbara said when I asked her to teach me what she knew about owls. "We admire her ability to see that which we cannot—indeed, to see in the darkness. But you should know that, as much as her ability to see is remarkable, her ability to hear is equally as strong. Most people do not know this.

"If you have been instructed by the Snake Goddess to let owl assist you, then this is a journey you must take alone, without my influence. I will tell you a few things, those that I found most intriguing. After spending much time exploring owls, what I came to admire the most was the way in which they handle sound.

"They listen first with one ear, then with the other, turning their head over and over toward the sound until they can hear it. Indeed once owl hears, she catches her prey. This seems to me an important teaching.

"Look," she went on, dropping down to the base of a tree. "You see this?" She broke apart a tightly wadded bundle of fur and tiny bones. "This is one of owl's pellets. These are what she ate but could not digest and so wadded up and released. These you should look for in your search for owl. Rarely is owl found by looking up. Look to the ground for pellets or feathers. Follow her trail, Aureillia."

Every day, after my exercises with Barbara, I would walk the forests in search of an owl. I spent many nights sleeping beneath trees beside which I had found her distinct pellets. I listened, one ear open for hooting, but I found not one.

I slept beneath the fig tree outside the Cave of Lifegiving Woman for so many nights that the priestesses finally invited me in. I was honored to be able to enter this sacred chamber of new life. There was a delicate stream traveling through it, making a rhythmic flowing sound.

The priestesses were ever so warm and welcoming.

They said owls did come there, but only very rarely. I reminded them that one had come for me. They nodded their heads knowingly. I understood.

The women bringing forth gave me such inspiration. Courageously enduring the pain of their body opening as a child descended within them, spreading them wider until they surrendered themselves to this pain, releasing into the world new life.

I had not felt the harsh reality of people's perceptions of me until I entered this cave. The longer I stayed, the more apparent it became that most of the women bringing forth were upset by my presence within the cave. They interpreted it as a stroke of ill luck for the child within them emerging. There were many looks in my direction preceded by whisperings. Their exclusion hurt me deeply; however, I respected their feelings and took my leave.

* * *

Inside my blue egg, my quilts wrapped around my feet, I try to shake off the fear that fills my being at the thought of returning to that place. I close my eyes and rock my body in deep breath. When I open my window I am surprised to find myself in a beautiful place. It is a field. A field of sacred herbs, much like ours here on Crete, except that this one is very hidden. Many tall trees encircle it. A woman walks in the field, a basket hung over her arm. She is gathering sacred herbs. She wears very dark and heavy clothing with a long scarf pulled up and over her head and face. She stoops to pick a flowering herb, looking around herself fearfully. She walks up to a hilly area and begins to turn rocks over, searching for something beneath them. She peels the bark off several trees, still looking around herself nervously. She places the basket inside the blanket, wrapping it up to look like any other bundle. She then walks down into the village. She keeps her eyes focused on the ground, stopping to speak only to those who speak to her first. As she gets farther into the village, I recognize it. It is the same dim, dark one I have visited before. In the center of the village is the place where the atrocities I have seen have transpired. No burnings or hurtings are occurring now, but their structures loom over the village as a foreboding reminder.

She walks farther, down a small dirt path beyond the town, finally entering a small wooden house. I am intrigued by this place. It is so very different from Crete. There are so many small buildings made out of wood. The people seem to live in a much more separated fashion than we do here. As the woman enters the house, she says something loudly. She removes her scarf. I recognize her instantly. It is she, the woman I have seen them hurt. These visions seem to be going back in time. She puts the basket of herbs under the table and enters another room where a child lies in bed, under many blankets. The girl sweats in fever. The woman wipes her repeatedly with a damp cloth. She returns to the kitchen and begins preparing tonics. She takes the remaining herbs and hangs them, upside down, among the clothing hanging in a small room. She goes in to her child and sits in a chair beside the girl, who must be her daughter. She presents the tonic to her in a fearful fashion, putting her fingers to her lips as if to signal the daughter silence in these matters. The child nods in acknowledgement and drinks the tonic quickly.

*　*　*

When I awoke from sleep one morning, there was a small silk packet beside me on the bed. I opened the purple silk and found the face of an owl carved so precisely into a piece of black obsidian that I knew it could only be the work of Danelle.

"How did you know?" I asked him when I found him in his workshop.

"Know what?"

"The owl. How did you know about the owl?"

"What owl?"

"Danelle, why did you send me this?" I asked, holding up the stone.

"Because something told me you would like it."

"Who told you?"

"Aureillia—what are you talking about?"

"Why is it that you decided to carve an owl?"

"Oh, one has decided to roost on the tree outside my window. All night long it speaks to me. One night it even came and sat upon my sill. We watched each other all night. What magnificent eyes they have."

"That sly little thing," I said. "You must take me to her."

For most of the following moon, I spent all my free time outside Danelle's room trying to see that owl. "You're crazy," he would say. "No owl is going to come with you sitting there waiting for it."

He was right, but I could not help myself. Still, I was able to explore its nest and its surroundings. It also gave me an excuse to see Danelle. I knew I was cheating, pretending to be waiting for an owl when in fact, it was Danelle I was waiting for. When I had reasserted my commitment to the Snake Goddess, I had vowed to eat every meal within the Center and spend every evening in silent meditation with Her. After my morning exercises and duties were performed, this left me with only a few hours of free time before I was due back at the temple.

Danelle knew of my commitment and never would have done anything to interfere, but he was just as happy to join me in breaking my own rules. We spoke not about what we were doing, though both of us were completely aware of it.

It seemed we could not get enough of each other during that moon. I would hear his footsteps coming down the path from the Center and I would run to the gate to meet him. We would fall into a passionate kiss, lasting all the way back to his room.

In the evenings I would leave the temple in search of him. I would always find him. He was always waiting for me. The nights I found him at Dolphin Cove were the finest. We would swim together and, like the dolphins, engage in endless caressing, our bodies moving to the rhythms of the waves. I loved kissing him when he was wet, the salt making him only that much more delicious, his slippery mouth sliding around inside mine.

"We are breaking your rule, Aureillia," he finally said to me one evening while we were sitting on the shore at the cove. "I am enjoying it so much that I have not said anything, but I fear now, as the time for your trance dance nears, that we are tiring you out too much."

I pulled his arms around my waist, leaned my head back into his chest and said nothing.

"I want to believe there will be something left of you when your work is done there," he said.

"Danelle, you're not waiting for me?" I said and as I said this, I realized that he was. "Oh, no. You must not," I said. "That would be too lonely."

"I'll do what is right for me."

"Danelle, don't be foolish. I could die in the next trance dance."

"Don't say things like that," he said angrily, standing up. "How can you say a thing like that? Don't you know that my biggest fear is to lose you?"

"Danelle, please," I said. "I spoke before thinking." But I was too late.

"You must not come to me anymore," he said. "Don't you dare to come to me anymore. Save yourself for your precious venom."

"But what about my owl?"

"It's not your owl, Aureillia. It is my owl."

The words hurt, but they were true. I had been unfair, lying to myself about too many things. I wanted him to wait for me. It was one of the only things keeping me moving forward. But I wanted to pretend to him that it did not matter to me. I wanted to let him go, in case he wanted to go. Now I realized that my dishonesty had only hurt him more. I needed him.

I was selfish. I knew. I was selfish and foolish but I could find no other way to be. I stood up and took a fistful of earth from the beach into my right hand and threw it with all my power into the sea. Then I filled both hands with earth and threw them angrily toward the sea. Then more and more and more, until the voice within me rose up and I began to shout.

"Why? Why must I do this? What good can come of this? Why must I give up my life to such horrors? It serves no purpose! This serves no purpose!" I collapsed into deep sobs upon the sand.

For the first time in many moons, I was Aureillia again.

# CHAPTER 15

Of course it was Danelle's owl. His talent had become known throughout the island. They were calling him a visionary.

Though he had decided to call them personalized signature stones, disavowing the sacred implication of the word, "amulet", he had indeed gone on to develop this craft.

People would come to see him. He would talk to them, walk with them, spend time with them. After they left, he would meditate upon them until he received an image. This image he would carve into a stone for them.

So many desired his skill. There were lists of people's names, all waiting. After he completed a stone, he would proceed to the next name on the list. He handled each with the same seriousness and intensity, working for long periods of time, allowing himself little rest.

As I had done so long ago, most of the recipients would have a hole drilled into the stone so that they could display them upon their chests from ropes hanging around their necks.

"Why must they insist on drilling holes into them?" Danelle would mutter. "And why is it that they continue to call them amulets when I have deliberately asked them not to?"

"Because amulets is what they are."

"I am an artist, not a magician."

"Can you not be both? They want others to see them. They feel them to be a form of self-expression, which indeed they are."

When I walked through Knossos or attended public events I was astounded by the number of people wearing them. Though each was different, they were instantly recognizable as Danelle's work.

Even if I did not know the person wearing one, I would often request a closer look. They would always agree, moving toward me excitedly and extending the signature stone within two hands.

After studying the engraving, admiring the work, I would look into the person's eyes and—behind the beaming pride—always see mirrored back at me the image captured in the stone.

It was remarkable. Danelle seemed to capture the part of themselves they held most dear.

Owl had come to him. Owl medicine he was using indeed.

For the rest of the moon, I tried to get my mind back on my work, but could not stop thinking about Danelle. How unkind I had been to him. How I longed for him. I dared not go to him, however, and continued to search the island for my owl. In that, too, I had no luck. By the time the rounded moon approached I was very low. I performed my trance dance with such little interest that the snake grabbed my leg, bit me, wrapped herself around me, and bit me again.

Barbara squeezed and squeezed until I screamed from the pain of her intensity. I began to shake and shiver. My heart pounding loudly within me.

"The egg. The egg. Aureillia," There was panic in Barbara's voice as my head fell backward onto the floor. She wiped my forehead with a damp cloth. She said again, more calmly this time, "Aureillia, try to get yourself inside your egg."

It was no use. I was unable to sit up and it had always been harder for me to create my egg from a lying down position. I could feel Barbara wrapping blankets around my legs. She handed me a piece of bread which I chewed very slowly. She held my hand tightly inside both of hers. I squeezed it back. "Stay here," she said. "Stay with me."

I am back in the house of my woman friend and her sick daughter. The daughter seems to be faring better, but I do not know the placement in time of the vision. The woman says something to her daughter, kisses her on the cheek, then puts the scarf over her head and goes outside. She walks through the village, up toward the field she had been in the last time I saw her. As she nears the row of trees at the edge of the forest, she looks up, and stands staring for quite some time. I look up too. That is when I see it: a large, great gray owl perched within the lower branches of one of those trees.

"I cannot believe it," I say to her. "I have been looking all over for you."

The owl regards me sternly. "It is not for you to look for me," she asserts.

"What are you doing here?"

"Sending a warning. Don't you need a place to sit? I see that your egg has not taken shape. I'm willing to let you borrow my branch."

I remain where I am, looking at her.

"Well, what are you waiting for?" she demands.

"How am I supposed to get up there?"

"Spread your wings and fly, silly bird."

"My wings?" I look down at myself: I have wings. I am all feathered, with claws for feet. I open my wings around myself in awe. I am an owl. "Oh, my," I say, attempting a smile but feeling a hardened beak in the place of my mouth. I spread my wings again, alarmed by how far they spread away from me. I hop and flap them clumsily in a repeated movement until I feel myself lifting off the ground. I feel an incredible feeling of lightness as I ascend higher and higher until I am able to rest and sail gently upon a current of air. I watch as the world below me becomes smaller and smaller. I alight next to the owl. From my perch I can see everything stretched out in front of me for a long distance. I see my woman friend, looking up at me, then around herself nervously.

"Why does she look so?" I ask.

"There is danger. What she is doing is unlawful."

"Unlawful? What is that?"

"It is forbidden."

"Forbidden? Why would that be?"

"It is considered a form of witchcraft."

"Witchcraft? What is that?"

"You ask too many questions."

"That is because I do not understand."

"You will understand what you need to understand when you need to understand it," the owl says. She spreads her mighty wings and flies silently away.

I watch her change from a huge winged creature into a small point on the distant horizon. I return my focus to my woman friend. How terribly strange it feels. I am required to move my whole head to change the focus of my vision. She is looking at me. She understands, but she proceeds into the forest in spite of my presence.

When she arrives home, the men in black are standing outside the door waiting for her. They take her basket and shake the contents of it onto the ground. They put her hands and feet in metal rings. They lead her away.

* * *

At the Cave of Mother Sea one day I said to Barbara, "I think I am ready. I think I have completed another set."

"Go ahead," she urged.

"Right here?"

"I can think of no better place," she said. She was sitting opposite me in the pool. Her hair was tied up high on her head, a few strands hanging into the water. She looked at me patiently.

"It does not make any sense," I said.

"Try," she said.

I closed my eyes, gathering my thoughts. "It seems there will come a time when it will be dangerous for women to do many of the things we do, like collect herbs for healing. Women will be hurt in a deliberate manner, after which they will be burned alive while others watch and do nothing to help them. These killings will be carried out by men in black cloth. Cats will also be thrown to their death upon these fires."

Barbara looked at me, her eyes open wide. "Did you get any determination of when this will all take place? Did it happen here, on Crete?"

"In my visions, I was not on Crete. There was no water nearby. It was a place much colder than here. The people wore very heavy, dark clothing. It seemed quite a different time than now."

"What could it possibly mean?" Barbara wondered.

"That is what I do not understand. I think that I have gotten all that I will of that story and yet—I ask myself, why? The poor woman deliberately hurt and burned alive for collecting herbs for her sick daughter."

"When my daughter was waning, I went to the field every day to make sure she would have the freshest herbs for the best tonic. I would even do things I knew would not work, only to feel that I was doing something for her. If I had not been able to do everything in my power to try to help her I would not have been able to tolerate it."

I shook my head. "I am so sorry," I said. "It must have been so very difficult."

"Difficult does not even come close to describing the loss of one's own child. Unbearable comes closer; unthinkable and never-ending pain," Barbara said, looking down into the water. Her pain came through it to reach me. I felt it enter me, an ache inside my bones.

"She was such a gentle child," Barbara said. "That is the thing I struggle the most with. Why? Why such a gentle child? Sometimes, I think her gentleness made her more vulnerable, more ethereal. Perhaps she was only meant to be here a short while; I do not know. The gentle ones do not seem to endure."

We sat there in the water, separately within ourselves. After a while Barbara looked up and said, "Please, continue."

I waited a while longer, then began, "At the end of my vision the owl took me up high. High into flight above everything so that I was looking down at a land mass with water around it. I did not know what I was looking at until I recognized a shape below it. It was the shape that the sea explorers have told us is the shape of Crete. It was there, also surrounded by water. If I saw what I think I saw then I must tell you that we are but a tiny bit of something very large. There are so many places around us and so many of them so much larger than our Crete.

"It gave me such a strange feeling. A feeling of being nothing and yet everything at the same time. I had never imagined such a feeling. The owl showed me the places of black smoke where the bodies of women were being burned. Indeed, there were many of them. My heart ached as we flew above this huge land mass north of Crete where, sometime in the future, they will burn the live flesh of women."

Outside, the sun was beginning to set. I watched the colors of the sky gradually change. "What could make people do such things?"

"Perhaps this is what you are meant to understand," Barbara said, "the reasons behind such cruelty. It cannot be a simple answer." She shook her head. "I must leave. I have become cold," she said, climbing out of the water.

When she stood up, I saw how thin she had become. The venom she had taken from me had indeed poisoned her.

"So very thin you are," I said to her. "How I worry about you."

"It is my job to worry about you," she said, covering herself.

Angered, I snapped, "It is for myself that I worry. I cannot finish my prophecies without your assitstance."

"I will try my best to see you through," she said, turning her back to me.

"I wish so much that I had not let you do that," I said desperately, standing behind her. "Oh, why did I let you do that? It is my fault that you are ill."

"You must not ever say that again," Barbara said, turning around and seizing my arm. "This was my mistake, not yours, Aureillia. We shall never speak of this again."

She exited the cave. I stood inside its black coolness listening to nothing.

# CHAPTER 16

The next moon, Barbara insisted that I go back to a more rigid routine. "I have a feeling things are only going to get worse for you where you go next," she said.

I knew in my belly that she was right. I was experiencing great resistance within myself about my next set of visions. I prayed harder and longer beneath the sculpture. As the rounded moon approached, Barbara had me out walking the beaches with her for long periods of time.

"You will need your legs to be strong," she kept saying. "You will need physical strength to endure it." On the beach we did breathing exercises over and over again. We began a new meditation, using the owl instead of the shell. I would be above the action looking on. Like the owl I would be a silent, passive observer. This appealed to me. I liked becoming winged, sitting up in a tree, now and then ruffling my feathers or going on a silent night flight.

I was glad when I saw what I had to see that she had done this extra work with me.

I dance the dance of the snake. She stings me in the crease of my arm so that it is difficult for Barbara to squeeze any venom out. She quickly drags me to my corner and tries to talk me up into my perch in the tree. But I cannot get myself up to the perch because the action is taking place inside a small grass hut. Such a thing I could never have imagined. Would that I had never seen it, then I would never have to report it. But see it I did and so, report it I must.

Being unable to get myself up into a tree, I burrow into the corner and take on the detached silence of my birdwoman self.

Wherever I am, the heat is incredible. Such a heat I have never felt. Though indoors, I can feel the sun's scorching brightness beating down. Inside the hut, a young girl is held down by four women. She is screaming. The screams become louder and louder, until they pierce my ears with a deafening sharpness, as a fifth woman takes what looks like a translucent dagger, and cuts into her sacred area with it. Into this young girl's most sacred spot she digs with that tool, tearing the flesh apart. The blood is everywhere.

I must have lost consciousness. When I awoke, the first thing I did was take my hands and immediately put them upon my sacred spot to see whether it was still in one piece. My fingers landed upon its whole smoothness, the lips still rounded and puffed, soft and moist to the touch. But unlike other times when my fingers would continue to explore, desire did not stir within me.

It was only then that I remembered the vision, like pieces of a most shocking and strange dream coming back to me. I sat up.

I was inside the temple. The breeze blew almost violently through the windows high above me. There was no one else near me. I could see evidence of Barbara, evidence of her silent and steady vigil beside me as I took my tour of horror. She must have been out collecting more herbs for a tonic or mushrooms for a broth. She was not there, and as she would have been the only thing to keep me there, I stood up and walked as best I could out of the temple. My stomach was twisted into many knots and my head pounded. I walked, hunched over myself and very slow, barely able to pick my feet up. That was when I remembered the last part of the vision, the part right before I had fainted.

After she had finished cutting the girl, that woman took a needle and some sort of thin string, and with the swift jerking movements of her hands, she sewed that girl's sacred area tightly together.

I leaned against the outside wall of the Center for a long time, trying to breathe. Eventually I gained enough strength to push myself along the wall slowly, one step at a time. Finally I reached the small dirt path that would lead me to the Cave of Mother Sea. There was nothing else in my mind but submerging myself into Her watery warmth. If I was tired and simply sank myself into Her for eternal bliss, I would not have minded that either. Though the sun was high up in the sky, giving us a beautiful day in the middle of the rainy season, to me it mattered not. I crawled along the little dirt path, my hands and knees dragging me forward. When I reached the sloping hill in the middle of the path, I felt two arms wrap around me from behind. It was Danelle.

"What is the meaning of this, Aureillia?" he asked.

I burst into horrifying sobs of such intensity that I feared I would scare him away. "Oh, Danelle," I cried, turning toward him, "I am so tormented. You will never know."

"Aureillia," he said, sitting down and rocking me within his arms.

But I picked my head up and looked at him. The scene, what we were experiencing at that moment, seemed eerily familiar. "Danelle," I said, "this, what is happening right this very moment, this is a fulfillment of a vision I had so long ago, in my youth."

"When I saw you through the window," he said, "I thought it looked like something you had once described to me."

"Oh, no," I said, beginning to shake with fear. "Do you know what this means?"

"What?"

"This means that the other visions that I have seen will also come to pass."

"You have not told me of your other visions."

"And I will not. Do not ever ask me to," I said. "Please, help me to stand."

Barbara was in a frenzy when she finally found me in Danelle's room later that day. I lay in bed and listened to them talk outside the window. I was surprised at how absolutely she trusted him. Feeling graciously protected, I fell asleep.

* * *

I found myself recovered in time for the bull leaping festivities. Minoa had long been known for its bull leaping. It served no purpose except to offer pure fun to the residents of Knossos. The festival of the bulls came at the end of the rainy season, when the people of Minoa were growing restless from being shut indoors. The community leaders decided this was a good time to provide raucous entertainment lasting from midday to the sun's set for one full lunar cycle. Villagers returned to their rooms feeling tired and happy. By the time the festival was over, the planting season had arrived and the rains had ended and there was much work to do.

Within each festival there were favorite leapers whom the crowd would wait for and demand to see over and over again through incessant chantings of their names. The festival included other activities: small wooden bulls set up for children to try out, larger ones for adults to learn on, special meals taken together, and dancing.

Barbara ordered me to take a moon's respite and attend as many activities as I could. "Plain enjoyment is what you need," she said. "You have been working yourself too hard."

I was reluctant. The last vision had left me cold. I did not think that I had much use for fun, but I knew I had to obey her orders.

Each day Barbara and I would do our exercises in the mornings. After midday meal, Danelle would be waiting for me outside the temple door and we would then go to the central court to watch the bull leaping together.

Sometimes Barbara would join us, never remaining seated with us for long. There were so many people she knew who all wanted her to sit with them. She hopped around that central court like a frog. I gave up trying to keep track of her and contented myself with sitting beside Danelle.

Occasionally, I would sit with Sheena, Hypia, or Thela. It was wonderful to see Leida, who was a girl already. She kept her distance, seeming rather afraid of me. I tried to remember what I had thought of Snake priestesses when I was young and not become upset by it. More than Leida, it was the way Sheena, Hypia, and Thela looked at me that made me uncomfortable. In fact, I had not realized how truly dreadful looking I had become until I saw the way people who had not seen me in a while looked at me. Though they tried to hide it, their faces were full of concern and pity.

In Danelle's eyes I never saw that. Perhaps because he, of all of them, had been going through this with me, seeing me deteriorate a little at a time, but I knew it was more than that. And so it was that I sat through the games holding his hand ever so tightly, hoping he would never let me go—the one person still connecting me to this world.

I was not surprised to learn that Katya had become one of the favorite leapers of the festival. Many days began and ended with chantings of her name. They wanted her first, they wanted her last.

Her leaps were certainly a sight to see. She leapt over that bull with amazing energy and enthusiasm, landing in a perfect standing position. She wore bright red and black clothing that swirled through the air as she leapt, a huge smile beaming on her face. One even got the feeling that the bull liked her. She was fire.

One night after the leaping I went to see her.

"It is so very good to see you again," she said, taking my hands into her own. I had forgotten how small she was, so large she looked in the court. "How pale you are. Are you quite all right?"

"The work is difficult," I said, relieved that she had dared to ask, "but it will soon be ended. I only hope to do it well. Oh, Katya, how enchanting you are out there."

"You poor thing," she said, not letting the subject go. "No wonder you feared them so. I barely recognize you as the same person."

All at once I was struck by an image of myself, myself in the vision which had recently come to fulfillment. The image of me crawling toward the Cave of Mother Sea. I remembered how horrified I had been by my own appearance in that vision when I had seen it as a girl. It occurred to me, as I stood there speaking to Katya, that that was exactly what I looked like. I was overcome with anxiety and felt I could not breathe.

"Aureillia, what is it?" Katya asked.

"Excuse me. I must go," I said, fleeing the court.

Danelle followed me. "Aureillia," he said, stopping me in the corridor. "Come, let's walk among the trees. The moon is white and half round."

I hesitated. I had not wanted to be alone with him outside the temple since my last vision. Every night, he walked me back to my room in the Center and kissed me gently on the lips before leaving me there. It was as though he could sense my hesitation, my dread.

"Come," he said to me now. "Just for a walk. Don't worry."

I followed his hand, which pulled me out into the wonderful freshness of the night air. We walked slowly, silently, beside each other along the paved walkway where trees bent over us in graceful gesture and the moon followed us, slipping her light through the spaces between their branches. It was cool and damp, clean and pure.

"Danelle," I said, finally, "I don't know how to say this." I led him off the path and into a group of trees. "I am sorry." I grappled for words, my hands rose in frustrated gesture. How could I explain to him what I was feeling without revealing information? "I'm having a difficult time," I faltered, starting again.

"It is not necessary to say anything," he said.

"But I only wish I could tell you, it would be so much easier if I could only give you some information."

"We need not speak of it," he said. "You are not obligated to me in these matters."

I leaned into his chest. His shirt was soft and warm against my face.

"Danelle," I asked, in earnest, "Why are you so good?" He laughed, shrugging off the question, until he saw my seriousness.

"Perhaps because I have good reason," he said.

People traveled from all over to see the Minoan bull leaping. The bull leapers worked tirelessly throughout the annum to create a variety of shows for the attendees.

The show started out with a series of dances performed by the leapers, some with leapers dressed as bulls, dancing between them, some performing acrobatics. The series of opening dances always ended with all the dancers on the floor spinning circles within circles—long lengths of silk held between them—until they became many colorful wheels spinning within each other. These spinning circles brought the energy in the court to a very high level for the leaping.

Then the bull was brought in. He had been denied food all morning. When he was led in to the court, he was offered a meal. Since he had not eaten, he devoured it ravenously, stuffing himself. This made him placid and passive and thus more useful in the leaps.

Each leap consisted of three leapers, one in front of the bull for distraction, another behind, and the leaper herself. The leader and follower worked very hard as a team to keep the bull moving at the proper pace for the leaper, who would have to judge her distance and begin running for the mount before he arrived at the meeting point. If the leader felt the bull was going too fast, she would signal to the one behind, who would shout to the bull or grab at him to slow him down.

Sometimes, the bull would charge. The leapers, in combined effort, would distract him from one another as they vaulted out of the court into the escape holes. The bull would be left running off his anger alone inside the court, whose walls were too high for him to get over.

Of course, the main attraction were the actual leaps themselves. The leapers would run toward the bull, jump up, and push themselves off his back high into the air, where they would perform several flips, somersaults, or other acrobatic tricks. Each had her own style, legs extended or held tight in to the chest. As the leaping progressed, the leaps became more intricate and daring. The show grew more exciting as it went on.

There were favored bulls as well, but in this the crowd could not have their own way. The leapers were the ones putting themselves at risk. They saved the privilege of choosing bulls to themselves.

Though I had originally resented Barbara's order, she had been right—the games had restored me. Simply being present in an atmosphere of excitement and fun, witnessing other people enjoying themselves, penetrated my being, sparked me back into a state of joy. By the end of the festival I had begun chanting as loudly as the others around me, looking excitedly toward the games all through the morning and rushing to the court for a good seat. Toward the end it was I who took Danelle by the hand, leading him deep into the forest where I pleasured myself upon him under a covering of thick and bending trees.

 **CHAPTER 17**

Barbara knew that I was anxious about the approaching trance dance. The festival of the bulls had helped, however, as the moon grew into roundness, my body became rigid with fear.

Barbara presented me with a relaxant tonic to drink for two days before and on the morning of my trance dance. Because the snake had a difficult message, Barbara held her steady as I danced, presenting her with my arm. She wanted her to bite me on the place on my arm where there was an abundance of tissue, exactly between my elbow and my wrist, that she may be sure to be able to squeeze a good amount of venom out.

It took some work, getting her to bite me in this manner, but it was well worth the effort, for as Barbara works patiently on removing some of the venom, I am remarkably present, sitting up watching, even able to walk to my pillow and remain in a seated position throughout the vision.

"Can you get up onto your perch?" Barbara asks.

I shake my head no. I am already back inside that hot grass hut.

"Are you an owl?"

I nod my head yes. I am burrowed into the corner again, camouflaged against the straw.

The girl I saw last time is sitting inside the hut with several other girls similar in age and appearance. They are all seated leaning against the wall, their legs extended straight in front of them, tied together. The fabric that holds their legs together is woven from a combination of colors of a brightness and beauty I have not seen before. There is a smell. A pungent, ripe smell.

A woman enters the hut, the one I saw perform the mutilation. She carries a basin of water with which she cleanses them all, untying their legs one at a time, inspecting their wounds, shaking her head in approval, smiling at them.

When she has finished attending to them all, she orders them to stand. It is clear from the expressions on their faces when they begin to move that it causes great pain. They make a grand effort at it, seeming to not want to let the pain show.

She lines them up within the hut. Not a word has passed from any of their mouths. It seems to take all of their concentration simply to move. On their faces is a shared expression of shock—a look I recognize—similar to the one I imagine to be on my face. Souls buried deep, beneath wide, wondering eyes; the face of silent knowing; the expression of an owl.

Out of the hut she leads them. In the straight line she has formed, they follow her, winding as a snake through the village. Their walk is slow. They do not lift their feet, but rather drag them slowly behind themselves. Some of them begin to bleed. Blood runs down their legs, leaving a spotted red trail upon this dusty brown soil.

Perched in a tree now, I am able to observe this village. A village of grass huts gracefully bordering a deep blue sea. The intense heat I had experienced within the hut was coolness compared to out here where the sun is able to reach me. The people seem accustomed to such heat. They go about their business as though it is a normal condition they live with. The astounding use of color I saw on the fabric within the hut continues throughout the village, in the clothing, the baskets, the pottery. It must be the influence of the strength of the sun here.

A drum beats as the girls are led through the village. People stop working in the fields and clap and sing as they walk by. Some take a moment to dance. All are acknowledging these girls, their faces smiling in pride toward them.

*   *   *

I was nearly not ill when I awoke. It was a relief to get up the next day with only a dull headache and an inability to eat for a few days before returning to my daily routine. I was again bothered by what I had seen, trying desperately to make sense of it. My mind raced and spoke itself into circles and corners but, still found no answers.

One night, while meditating beneath the great arms of the Snake Goddess, the voice said, "Owl has taught you all she will for now. You need dolphin medicine. In this you must waste no time."

My first instinct was to gather up Danelle and have him lead me through this journey. But as I thought about it, I realized that most of my experiences with dolphins had been filtered through Danelle. Because they were his familiar, I had made the foolish assumption that they were only for him; much the same way I had assumed the owl was only for me. I suddenly understood that unless a person has her own relationship with something, she will never know how it is that certain thing desires to speak uniquely to her.

I was unsure how to go about it, as I was timid about entering the water alone. I stood within her edges at Dolphin Cove, letting the water lap my toes, but dared not enter. No dolphins came. I decided to try mornings. Every morning for a week I woke up early and went down to Dolphin Cove to try to see them following the fishing boats returning from their sunrise runs. I was right, there were dolphins, but there were also children, calling to them and swimming with them much as I had done in my youth. This would not do. The children could not understand what I was doing there, looking at me suspiciously; and I could get no time alone with the dolphins, who were far more interested in the children than they were in me.

A few days later, I went down to the marina to see whether there was a small boat I could borrow. I was directed to a fisherman named Aubrey whom many said knew the most about dolphins.

Aubrey was a large man. He let the hair on his face grow, covering and hanging from his chin. He was very friendly, even offering to take me around and show me the dolphins' favorite spots.

"Of course," he said to me one day as we traveled the contours of the island in his small boat, "the best way to get to know the dolphins is to swim with them."

"Yes," I said, "I know that to be true. But where?" He smiled and turned the boat into a cove I was not familiar with. It was very wide and quiet, encircled by jagged rocks reaching into sheer cliffs upon the hills surrounding it.

It seemed the only way to arrive at this cove was by boat. While still far from shore, the boat suddenly came to a stop, its bottom scraping against soft sand. Aubrey got out of the boat and looked at me, laughing. The water was reaching to a spot below his knees. It was quite remarkable: in the middle of the deep waters, a large area where the sea had moved enough sand to create a hill within the water. "The dolphins love it here," he said, "and when they come here, they are very much in the mood for playing."

He laughed a loud, hearty laugh. I felt I was not grasping his meaning. I got out of the boat and stood beside him, the water reaching up to just above my knees.

"This is perfect," I said, feeling ever so grateful to him. Here I could be alone with the dolphins while feeling safe within the shallow water. Aubrey agreed to let me use his boat in the afternoons. "You must see this place on the rounded moon," he said.

Simply being in the water was helping me to feel better. Every free afternoon, I borrowed that boat and rowed myself to that sand hill. For days I swam alone, hesitant at first, but soon my fear dissipated. I rolled in the water, laying my head back, face toward the sky. I sat in the boat nibbling upon fruits, sitting silent time, even sleeping in the warmth of the sun, so good to feel after all that rain. No dolphins came.

As the moon grew into roundness within the sky, they began to come, more of them each day. They swam in circles around my boat. It rocked boisterously upon the waves of their movement. I sat in the boat and watched their sleek, shiny gray bodies maneuver gracefully through the water.

Finally, after persistent beckoning from them, I got out of the boat and stood on the sand hill. The water splashed around my knees as they swam circles around me. One of them was particularly friendly. He circled and circled, nudging at my legs with the whole side of his body, almost pushing me over until I submerged myself in the water and began to swim with him. He swam along beside me, calling out in his high-pitched whistle. Then he grasped me with his flipper, lifted me up high into the air so that I was far above the water, and flipped me over so that I fell swiftly back into the water with a loud slap. I tried to swim away, to recover my breathing, so shocked was I, but he gripped me once again, this time flipping me higher in the air. My whole body twirled and flipped in the open air as I descended back toward the water, entering it with such force that it stung my skin. Before an effort could be made to try to breathe, he seized me again, flipping me yet another time. I surrendered, allowing my fright to turn into laughter as he sent me sailing higher and even farther through the air. With this laughter came the breath for which I had been struggling. Something within me broke free and I opened to this game and joined him in pure play.

The time for my trance dance had arrived. I rowed the boat toward what I knew would be my last visit to the sand hill until I was well recovered. It could be any number of days or even longer than that. I was frustrated by this thought. Just when the dolphins had started to come. As my boat touched down, I was immediately met by a dolphin swimming frantic circles around it. I stepped out into the soft sand. He pulled me into the water with his flipper so that I lay against the sand on my back. He began pushing his firm sacred limb against me. I was astounded by his assertiveness. I turned and tried to swim away, but he continued to push himself against my back as I moved through the water. I stood up and firmly extended my arms, my hands open toward his head.

"No," I commanded.

He responded, circling slowly around me in defeat. I sat down in the shallow water. He came to be next to me. I rubbed him gently on the back and top of his head with my hands, the sun reflecting up into my eyes from the clearness of the water around me.

Barbara has done a good job controlling the bite of the snake again. I sit up on my pillow. I become the bird woman. I can tell, even before the vision becomes clear, that I am in a different place. I know immediately because the heat—the glaring sun—is gone. I am in a room. It is very clean. There is no presence of dirt. There is nowhere for an owl to burrow herself into. All the things around me are as cold and hard as stone, but they are not stone. They are a silver color, smooth to touch, some kind of shaped metal. There is a high platform upon which sleeps a young girl. She is very pale and still. I begin to wonder whether or not she is alive. There are several men around her, dressed in bright white cloth. This white cloth is also tied around their mouths, strangely showing only their eyes. One of the men takes a knife, which he aims at her sacred spot. I cannot bear to see this again. I am growing agitated. I can hear myself muttering as, in the distance, Barbara's hand seizes my own. I hold on to it as they open the girl up, not cutting into the lips this time. Two of the men have their hands on either side of her sacred spot.

They spread the lips wide to expose a piece of flesh hanging down from the topmost section. It is this that, with the knife, the other one removes.

*   *   *

Though not sick when I woke up, I did not arise from bed. I lay there for days, not speaking. When I did finally get up, I kept to myself, not wanting to be near anyone. I sat in silence, watching the days go by. I knew I should return to the dolphins, but I avoided it. I avoided thinking about the reasons why I avoided it. Anger grew within me. I sent Danelle away when he came to me. I spoke to no one. In meditation one night, the Goddess whispered into my ear, "Go to them. You will see. They will help you."

The next day I walked to the port.

"Good morning," Aubrey said, greeting me. "Where have you been? I've been expecting you for weeks."

"I know." I shrugged.

"A little too much for you?"

"What do you mean?"

"Most people are surprised by the dolphins' activities."

I felt angry and defensive, but I said nothing.

"On the other hand," he continued, "maybe you were not, since you have come back at the time when they begin to be the most active," he said, pointing to the sky. "Like us."

I tilted my head to the right. I had not made this connection.

"While we are busy on the mountain, they are busy in the water."

I rowed my boat to the sand hill, becoming angrier with each lift of my arms. "Why?" I called out to the Snake Goddess. "Why are you making me see all of this now? Why must I come here?" I sat in my boat, my arms hanging over the edges, my face close to the water. No dolphins came.

The next day I returned. I had been thinking about what Aubrey had said, about the rounded moon celebrations. My head had been dizzy with want of understanding. The dolphins arrived suddenly. I removed my clothing and went into the water. None of them seemed particularly interested in me. They allowed me to swim with them, within them, between them. I moved my body in long sensuous movements like theirs, trying to make the movement originate from my hips, my arms stretched high in front of me, hands clasped. They swam around me, tirelessly caressing each other, rubbing their smooth bellies together. I was surprised to observe how much time the male spent around the female's sacred area, fondling it with his fin, pushing his nose inside her as she squealed with pleasure.

I watched them. I tried to hear what it was they wanted to tell me.

The time drew nearer to the rounded moon. The dolphins became more and more active, more excited. One day while I swam with them, one of them approached me, rubbing up against me over and over, nudging at my arm with her sacred spot in invitation. "No," I said, swimming away. "Absolutely not. Go find one of your kind."

But she followed me, her whistle increasing in tone and intensity as she continued to push against me persistently. I extended my fingers to touch her. She was soft and warm, curling herself in pleasure as I opened her. Within her enveloping folds, my fingers found it toward the top, hardened and protruding. She had one too. I said it out loud, without realizing I was speaking. "You have one too!"

The dolphin turned and looked at me. She stared straight into my eyes with hers—big and black—until I heard it. Then she swam away.

The next day I went to the temple of Female Being.

Two of the priestesses sat down with me for a private inquiry. They had a name for it. They said if I had not been a priestess in the temple of the Snake Goddess, I would be more familiar with it.

"Most women begin to experience it at the rounded moon ring dances on Moon Mountain. That is when a woman is most open to the Gift of the Goddess."

"The Gift?"

"Oh, yes. That is what it is called. The Gift of the Goddess."

"Why is it called that?"

"Because it serves no other purpose except to offer a woman pure pleasure. Therefore, it has always been thought that it must have been a gift."

I told them about my experience with the dolphins. They were familiar with this. They advised me to go to a rounded moon celebration. "At the dances," one of them said, "paticipants are able to experience a heightened sense of pleasure. Some are even able to transcend into ecstatic trance."

"Could you tell me," I asked hesitantly, "Why would anyone ever want to remove this part of a woman?"

They did not act shocked, which surprised me. They nodded their heads gravely. "We have heard of this beginning to happen in the land to the east of us."

"Now?"

"Yes, now. I have even see a woman who has had this done to her," the priestess said, shaking her head in dismay. "How is it that you know of this?"

"I cannot say," I said, but my hand instinctively moved to the place on my arm of my last bite. They shook their heads and asked no more.

"Only, I wonder," I continued, "if you could think of any reason why someone would do that?"

"We discussed this matter at length after having met that poor woman," the first priestess said, looking toward the other one. "We decided the only reason would be to deny a woman the pleasure the Goddess has given to her. Why they would want to deny a woman her pleasure, however, we do not know."

I bade the priestesses farewell. I was terrified by their suggestion to attend a Moon Mountain celebration. The thought of sacred touch turned me cold inside.

"Of course, they're right," Barbara said when I told her that I had been advised to go. "You should attend. It is too late for me to release you for this moon, but you may have the following. It will be a nice change for you."

This house is extreme in its difference from the houses here on Crete. It is made of wood. It must not be a windy place, for the windows are large and placed in the center of the walls. There are a lot of things in this house. The rooms seem to overflow with things. There is a woman helping a child into bed. She pulls the covers up to her neck and kisses her on the forehead. She leaves the room, closing the door behind her. The girl kicks the blankets off and gets up and walks over to a window. She opens the window and looks for a long time outside, where it is still daylight. In her face is longing. I recognize her: it is the young girl I saw in my last vision, the one sleeping on the table. The one from whom the men in white removed her Gift. She still has it now, however, for she lies in bed with her legs spread wide and enjoys it. The door opens suddenly. The woman enters. She sees the girl. Anger covers her face as she screams something. The girl, sitting up, has backed against the wall that her bed sits next to. She holds her hands behind her, her face filled with fear. After much coaxing, she places them upon the railing at the bottom of the bed. She closes her eyes and drops her head, sobbing, while her mother whips them until they bleed.

"I think I am ready," I said to Barbara. The sun was shining down upon her face, reflecting the redness of her hair back toward her. She smiled. She seemed almost alight. We were sitting in the field of sacred herbs. We were both excited about taking a moon off and having finished another set of visions.

"All right," she said, sitting up taller. "Go ahead." I took a deep breath. I had been thinking a long time about this, how to say it. I looked up toward the blue sky, then closed my eyes while still looking up, so that redness pushed against the outside of my closed eyelids.

"There will come a time when women are not allowed to enjoy the Gift of the Goddess," I said. I breathed deeply, and squeezed my eyes shut more tightly, continuing, "They will be scolded if they pleasure themselves upon it. It will be removed with a knife or sharp rock. In some instances only the Gift shall be removed; however, others will find it necessary to cut and mutilate the entire area down to the bone."

Barbara looked at me for a long, hard moment. The color had suddenly drained from her face. Saying nothing, she stood up and vomited behind a row of trees.

# CHAPTER 18

On the center point of the day of the rounded moon, there are circle dances on Moon Mountain. Inside the stone circle, anyone who has been initiated may participate in the celebration of Her full, life-giving roundness.

Each time the moon is round, residents of Knossos sleep during the light hours and spend the dark time awake in celebration. It was not customary for a Snake priestess to attend, since trance dances occur at rounded moon time.

I was one of many people walking up the well traveled dirt path of this so-often climbed hill between the Center and the sea. It was freeing to see that here, on Minoa, people were engaged in celebration, unaware of the knowledge I possessed.

The moon was out and shining Her large fullness, seeming to follow behind me as I walked toward Her place of worship. Her light filled the darkness: an enchanting silver light, a light containing moisture.

I could feel the plants around me reaching, the flowers stretching their long, graceful velvety necks toward Her. I could hear their faint, almost inaudible buzzing. I could see the tallest trees expanding, their leaves alert and listening. I knew that most of their growth happened in the dark, by the light of the moon, but I had never witnessed it so completely. Whereas the sun's light is sharp and pounding, forcing us to seek respite, the moon's light is moist and nourishing—a softer light to reach ourselves toward, a safer light to embrace.

Minoans of the past built this wide circle on the flat, grassy top of this hill from thirteen tall, rounded gray stones. Each stone is aligned with its own moon, whose light reflects off it at the center point of its rounded time. When Her light shines off Her moonstone, the celebrations begin.

I remove my garments, leaving them outside the circle of stones. Bathed in Her particular light, as She created me, I enter Her circle. Upon the damp grass I sit among others in stillness.

Energy bounces back and forth among the stones, humming. My body tunes itself to this energy, a much higher energy than I am accustomed to. From the base of my spine up through the crown of my head I can feel every part of my body reaching up toward Her milky light; stretching, extending. I feel a surge of power—an energy from my core, from that place within me that matches Her, radiating outward to meet Her.

Light flashes, reflecting off Her moonstone across from me, sparking instant, loud drumming. We stand and form circle within circle within circle. Hands joined we begin a ring dance, spinning, arms once raised, once lowered, first one way, then the other. Pulse quickens, inside a steady pounding begins, breathing deepens. The speed of the spinning increases as we circle, stop, circle again. Heat rises within the stones from the intensity of the whirling, from the presence of many bodies, more of which join all the time. The circle widens, becomes thick with heat, the drumming grows faster, louder, more urgent with each beat as we continue to spin, stop, spin again. Spin, stop, spin again until the movement becomes confused and we fall out of the ring dance.

Broth is passed around, broth of the poppy, sweet sacred nectar which we drink, which we feed into each other. There are no leaders here, there are no followers, only those who wish to enjoy the fullness of Her presence, the whiteness of Her light, the union of bodies in pleasure.

The broth releases in us the dance that is present, of ourselves creating long, slow, singular movements that lead to other movements. The beat of the drum slower now, slow steady beat upon which we ride, movement upon movement, sway, rock. Dew covers skin, stretching—awake with damp longing.

Skin meeting skin. Contours meeting curves. Wanting hands reaching (tingling) waiting breasts rising to fingers stroking (feeling) open mouths seeking ripe round heads, stems growing taller (thicker, wider) tasty droplets releasing. Warm folds swelling to each other exploring (rocking, swaying) upon hardened stems protruding. Hips opening to hips (widening, spreading) entering deeply (each other) more deeply entering (pushing, thrusting) dancing moving (together feeling). Drumbeat increasing, bodies releasing. Silvery white feathered wings raising (around extending) fluttering shuddering lifting to flight.

CHAPTER 19

I spent much time alone in my boat, sitting and watching the dolphins circle and play around me. Anger swelled within me. I did not go in with them. I wished I could be one of them. Dolphins do not possess knives. The same question rambled though my mind incessantly, repeating tirelessly, like a dull ache. *Why? Why? Why?* Why would anyone want to take it away? To steal the gift of pleasure from a woman?

No answer presented itself to me. I wandered the beaches, aimlessly looking about me. I slept alone beneath the trees, praying for a dream. I entered the pillar crypt, but still no answer came to me.

The feelings I grappled with I had never before encountered. Feelings of meaninglessness, desperation and loss of will. Terrified by my own isolation, I decided to conduct a cleansing fast. For three days and three nights, no food entered my mouth—only fresh, cool water. I became weak, my head tightened around itself, my body hollowed itself. I meditated beneath the sacred sculpture until my legs grew numb.

I have entered the darkness and I cannot find my out. I have entered the darkness and I cannot find my way out.

These words reverberated inside my empty self until I finally collapsed during meditation, landing, awake, upon my side, with my ear to the floor. I closed my eyes, begging for sleep to take me.

"Dolphin has taught you all she will for now," the voice said. "Go back to Moon Mountain. The council of elders awaits you."

On the new moon, and for the period of three days of darkness before She shows herself once again in the sky as an ever so thin silver crescent, the council of elders keeps vigil upon Moon Mountain, awaiting Her return.

Only members of the council and invited guests are welcome. I was not surprised to have received my invitation in this manner.

It was the stars that guided my way toward Moon Mountain this time. The path that was so bright and busy at the rounded moon was now dark and empty. The plants seemed to sleep in stillness with the moon. I walked cautiously, following my feet slowly through the darkness.

Within the stone circle a large fire burned high. The council of elders and other guests sat around it. They motioned for me to also find a place to sit. I sat myself down within the circle. The fire sparked reflections off the stones surrounding it—flashing once here, once there, alternating from stone to stone.

Each night began with chanting that lasted for a long period of time: until the energy between the stones was raised to an audible level.

I was fascinated by how, through the use of our voices combined with the light bouncing back and forth among the stones, we were able to heighten the energy within the circle to the same level as the night of the rounded moon.

After the chanting, the seeds of the poppy were passed around. These were eaten to facilitate communication with those from other planes of existence. It was at new moon vigils that wisdom was sought. It was here that the council of elders brought forth questions they could not answer on their own.

During the first two nights, I observed in awe as council members conversed with beings I could not see. I would sit and observe as they entered an altered state and began responding to a presence I could not perceive.

On these nights it was I, and others not at the time involved in trance state, whose responsibility it was to keep the fire burning high and the food circulating, for even while in trance the elders continued to eat.

During the hours of light we slept under the shade of nearby trees or bushes, gathered firewood, and prepared food for the night ahead. A great deal of wood was needed to keep the light burning bright through all the hours of darkness. The work was intense. Darkness returned quickly.

On the third night, when the chanting was completed, I sat sucking the bitter juices out of the seeds of the poppy and staring at the red and yellow tongues of flames crackling before me.

"Be not afraid of the darkness," someone said to me. "It is darkness that shall lead you to the light."

I looked around the circle until one of the wise women elders nodded her head and smiled at me. It was she who had spoken, planting her words within my head without making a sound. Her face held mine in magnetic trance. Though I tried, I could not move my vision from her. Her form became muddled and blurry. I thought it was my own vision that was faltering, but then I realized that it was her. She was actually changing form. Her face was dissolving, melting. Her whole body contorted and twisted as it shifted shape. I had never witnessed such a thing; her face actually became the face of another.

Sitting there before me, in the place that only a short time earlier had been a member of the council of elders, now sat my grandmother, my mother's mother, as I had last seen her—Rory. There she sat, the same strong nose and eyebrows as Sheena, with a long braid of white hair hanging to one side of her head.

"Rory," I said. "What are you doing here?"

"It is you who has called upon me," she replied.

"I did?"

"Yes, and it has certainly been a long journey back," she said, smiling slyly. "The elders tell me that it is time you learned the truth about me."

"The truth about you?" I repeated. I was surprised by this statement. I thought I had known the truth about Rory. She had been a sailor, spending most of her time journeying to faraway places on the large ships of trade.

In my youth, I used to love to sit in the central court of our block in the evenings and listen to her stories of distant lands. The ones that impressed me the most were the stories of the islands of Malta. She told of the remains of giant stone temples and underground chambers there.

Grandmother Rory said if one slept inside one of these underground chambers, the Goddess would grant them a dream or a vision. Whenever Rory and her fellow shipmates traveled in that area, they would spend the nights inside one of them. "Though abandoned by their builders long ago," Rory would say, "the Goddess is still there. She still speaks to all who enter there."

As a child, I had dreamed of journeying to Malta with Rory. I had imagined us sailing, her and I alone on a small boat. As we slept together within one of the underground chambers, the Goddess would whisper into our ears.

Rory was taken back when I was still a girl. We never were able to make our trip together, which made it even more special to have her sitting here before me now.

"To the south of us," she began, "were always women of great power and knowledge. When there were problems on Crete that we could not solve on our own, the priestesses of the Center would consult the council of elders. If no answers were provided after requests at three consecutive new moon vigils, it was time to seek assistance in the land to the south.

"There, the land had been peopled far longer than our Crete. The wise women were wiser, having had more years to aquire and pass on their knowing. Indeed, it was there that the Goddess brought herself into being—there that she brought forth from herself the first humans.

"At such times as these, it was I whom the council of elders would send out journeying in search of further assistance."

"Grandmother Rory," I said, "you were a priestess?"

"No, my dear. I did not have the honor of being a priestess. I was a seeker. At a young age I displayed a talent for languages. I could begin speaking in another tongue after hearing it only a few times. The elders recruited me as a seeker in foreign lands, for, in this task, proficiency in languages is the main skill required."

"Why have I no knowledge of this?"

"Discretion was utterly necessary, especially within my own community. Though I was a seeker in foreign lands, occasionally the elders required me to seek out information on Crete herself; within my own community. To seek out information is not only to ask but also to gather that which people might not want to tell. I was considered a sailor. This title assisted me greatly in performing my duty."

"Why has my mother not told me of this?"

"Your mother knows not. It would have placed her in too difficult a position. All know there is a seeker among them. All know they need seekers, but they also understand that they must not know who she is. If you think upon it for a while, Aureillia, you will understand the reasons why."

I looked at Rory. I tried to make her be what she said she had been, rather than what I had thought she had been. It was difficult.

"On my journeys, I met many interesting people. The most magnificent, however, were always the women to the south. Whenever we needed knowledge, they gave it willingly. Their wisdom was vast and far reaching, their generosity and grace were remarkable. They had an intricate and well designed network of communication among their villages. What one did not know, surely another did. Questions were sent from village to village until answers were forthcoming.

"They admired the talents of our artisans and remarked often on the 'inspired people of Minoa,' which made me proud. Many that I met I invited back as guests to our island. To those who came, I was able to return some of the warm hospitality I had received.

"In my later years, I fell into a spell of darkness much as you have now. Someone had passed me information that I found intolerable. Even after I passed it on, it stayed inside me, the pain and anger festering. I became very uncomfortable, roaming aimlessly, trying to find a way to cope.

"On a trip south at this time, the ship pulled ashore for an unplanned stop. Many of the people on board had become ill. We could not go on. We waited on shore as the healer of the village was called forth to help us and also to make sure we would not cause illness to her village with our presence.

"The healer's name was Zula. She emerged from the thickets onto the beach on which we waited. She wore a white dress tied neatly at the waist. Her hair, held away from her face by a large headpiece, cascaded in thick black curls down her back. I was drawn to her instantly. As I approached her, I was overcome with a feeling of familiarity—an intense remembering—which startled me.

"After tending to the sick crew members, Zula held her hand out to me. 'Come,' she said, 'You shall be my guest in the village.'"

"After a meal and much conversation, she turned to me almost suddenly, saying, 'This anger you carry possessively within you must be released. This piece of knowledge that you hold on to, it is this which makes you ill.'

"'I am to help you. You must learn the dance of release.' She moved closer to me and whispered, her dark eyes hypnotizing me with their depth, 'I knew that you would come. I was given a dream. We have known each other before. Can't you feel it?'

"I nodded my head, unable to speak.

. . ."'We were priestesses together', she continued, 'on the islands of Malta, when the temples were active.' At that moment, sitting there with Zula, all the pieces of my life fell together—all the fragments and parts lining up into one cohesive whole, which I could suddenly see clearly—and I knew that I could now continue; from there, I could continue on.

"For days, while the others recovered on the beach, Zula taught me the dance. I performed it over and over until it was certain that I had cleared myself. Then she introduced me to the Serpent of Fire. As a seeker, this knowledge was my greatest gift to Minoa."

"Serpent of Fire?" I said. I had never heard of such a thing.

"Yes, it is she who taught me about it, even making a trip to Crete later to teach others. You see, Aureillia, in my darkest hour I was given my greatest gift."

"Grandmother, you must tell me of this Serpent of Fire."

"This you shall discover on your own."

"Where?"

"Where She is sought so too is She found."

"Please, tell me something more about it."

"The Serpent of Fire is a journey one must take alone," she said, she was beginning to lose shape.

"Whom shall I ask? Please do not go!"

"Aureillia, do not let the pain become you."

"Grandmother Rory," I pleaded, but it was too late. The wise woman was shifting shape back into herself. There she sat before me, in the place that had been Rory.

 # CHAPTER 20

When I returned to the temple the first thing I asked, upon meeting Barbara, was, "Is there another serpent who is sacred to us?"

"Yes," she answered. "The venomless serpent whose power lies in Her ability to coil and uncoil. She who lies dormant within us until we awaken Her."

"Why do I not know of this?"

"Only those who ask are told."

"How is it that you came to know of it?"

"I have been engaged in a practice for some time now."

"Practice? What kind of practice? Where can I learn this practice?"

"Quiet yourself, Aureillia," she said, raising her hand toward me sternly. "These are the teachings of the high priestesses and priests. You must allow them to come to you."

"I must know. I cannot wait."

"In these things one has no choice. However, be consoled by the knowledge that where She is sought so too is She found," she said, echoing the words of Rory.

"But can you not tell me something of it?"

"The Serpent of Fire is something that must be experienced. It is a journey taken alone. I can tell you now that the Serpent of Fire appeared to me during one of my early trance dances. Indeed, the information I transmuted through my visions concerned a series of discussions with Her."

"This is what you discussed with the high priestesses and priests?"

"Yes, that's right. It is a relief to finally be able to tell you. It was difficult for me as a mentor not to be able to discuss my own work with the snakes. But that is the nature of the high teachings."

"How can this knowledge be kept a secret? It seems almost unfair."

"Not if you believe that people receive knowledge as they are ready for it, so that whoever is ready shall receive. If one is not ready, working with the Serpent of Fire is most frustrating."

"You knew nothing of Her before your vision?"

"Nothing." "Please, there must be something you can tell me."

"Yes, it is true," she said, thinking. "I can tell you first of all that She is beyond any description. She is the divine energy that fills the cosmos and also resides within us. You have already experienced Her in the moments you think of as 'divine union' or 'pure bliss.' She is always with us, always active. The practice only gives Her a name and allows one to become more conscious of Her."

I told Barbara about Rory and the healer Zula. She was intrigued by the story. "And it was she who told you of the Serpent of Fire?" She asked.

"Yes."

"You should be hearing from someone soon," she said, nodding her head, a faraway look in her eyes.

I knew the first thing I needed to do toward a sense of release: I needed to cut my hair.

It was very rare for a woman on Crete to cut her hair. Most wore theirs long, behind their ears, dangling loose, or in braids down their backs.

Mine had become horribly dry and thin from the venom. It had seemed to stop growing and become a lifeless form I carried around with me.

I closed my eyes as Barbara chopped away at it with a knife, cutting it close to my head. I looked in panic at the hair lying below me in piles upon the floor. Hair, the symbol of inner power manifesting itself in outward form. Thank goodness I still had the hair on my legs.

"You are a different person," Barbara said, observing me in awe. "It's remarkable."

Barbara's face became lighter, as though looking at my changed appearance offered her relief. I looked at myself in the reflective glass she held before me. My hair—thick and healthy, almost standing up on my head—bordered my face, which did, in fact, look much younger, more vibrant.

"What could happen to a person with such hair?" I said, but I was smiling.

I went to see Danelle. As I entered his block I saw him and, my long ago teacher, Tolles standing outside his room, speaking. Danelle leaned against the wall, his arms crossed in front of him, nodding his head in response to something Tolles was saying.

"Hello," I said to both of them, but mostly to Tolles, whom I had not seen in annums.

"Aureillia," Tolles said, clasping my hands within his, "I do not think I have ever seen such hair."

"Oh," I said, running my fingers through it so that it stood up within them. "I needed to make a change."

"You have certainly succeeded," he said.

"The change serves you well," Danelle said, putting his hands through my hair. "It has been some time since I have seen you look this radiant."

We stood talking for a while, when suddenly Tolles turned to me and said, "I hear you seek knowledge of the Serpent of Fire."

"Yes," I said, surprised. I had not made mention of it to Danelle. "How did you know?"

"I received notice," Tolles said.

"I do not understand your meaning," I said, looking to Danelle, who had an amused smile on his face.

"I would be most honored to be your teacher in these matters," he said, bowing toward me in sacred gesture.

"You?" I felt I might fall over in shock. Tolles a high priest? They were simply among us like this?

"Do not be so surprised, Aureillia," he said. "We are of all kinds."

"You are a high priest?"

"That is right."

"Why do I not know this?"

"You know it now," he said. "There was no need to know it before." He looked at Danelle. "There is something else," he continued, "while we are revealing things."

I looked at him. "Yes?"

"Danelle is one of my students. He has been engaged in a practice with the Serpent of Fire for some time now."

"Danelle?" I said. I was overcome. "You're always ahead of me," I said, looking at him angrily so that his whole face became a held-back smile.

"This is not a race, Aureillia," Tolles said.

"That's good," I said, still looking at Danelle, daring him to laugh, "because if it were, Danelle would always be winning."

They both laughed and I joined them, but I was desperately jealous and could not wait for Tolles to leave so that I could try to extract information from Danelle. But, hard as I tried, I could not get a word out of him. Though I teased and begged and told him he only had to nod his head one way or another, and therefore not speak any words, he still declined, holding his mouth in that reserved way he had.

"Aureillia, you will see Tolles tomorrow. Try to forget about it for now," he said, wrapping his arms around me and pulling me toward him.

But I would have none of it. I stormed away from him in anger, my frustration only increasing in the knowledge that as I walked away, he was watching me with a smirk on his face.

The next day I went to see Tolles in one of the high rooms of the Center. Only invited people were allowed in the upper levels. I had been here once before, with the council of elders, after my first oral prophecy. It was very quiet, removed from all the traffic and goings on in the lower Center. From the corridors of the upper level there was a magnificent view of the landscape surrounding the Center.

I stood and looked for a while at the view of the sea, ships afloat upon it, the landscape of the island cascading toward it. Of course, I had returned to Danelle after storming the entire length of this downhill terrain I looked upon now, and then stomping the entire uphill walk back. It was late and I was tired, but my anger had left me and he had been there, waiting for me at our meeting place. He had fallen asleep, so long had I kept him waiting. But this release, this release from walking . . .

My thoughts were interrupted by Tolles' hand upon my elbow.

"Wonderful view," he said.

"Yes."

"Come, we will walk toward where you look."

We walked together out of the Center down the path, toward the sea. I told Tolles about my night upon Moon Mountain and Rory.

"Yes. I have heard of her," he said, his hands behind his back. His stature was quite the same as when I had known him, small, thin and muscular. His hair, though still thick, was longer now. It framed his face, giving him a much more relaxed look, adding a suggestion of the wild and unusual that had not been there before. This was a different Tolles from the one I had known in my youth. He still had his calm demeanor and stillness, but there was a loosening about him that compelled me. What could cause this kind of change in someone?

"From what I know of your grandmother," he was saying, "and from what I remember of her, you seem to me quite like her."

"Do I?" I said. "Thank you, Tolles. I consider that a compliment."

"As well you should. Without Rory, or her teacher Zula for that matter, we would not have these teachings. It takes a great seeker to know which knowledge will truly benefit a community. The knowledge of the Serpent of Fire has added much to ours.

"There are only a few things that can be taught about the Serpent of Fire through the use of words alone. These I shall tell you now," he said, stopping and turning to me.

"The Serpent of Fire lives within everyone. You should know that she lies coiled at the base of the spine until she is awakened either by accident or through conscious activation. Conscious activation is what people attempt when they say they are engaged in a practice with Her. Some are successful, some are not. In all who are successful, activation leads to a reunion with the Goddess, the highest achievment one can hope for."

I stood looking at him anxiously.

"You are so very serious, Aureillia. Far too serious, I must say. I fear such seriousness will stand in your way."

"But I can only be what I am. This is ever so important to me."

"Why is it that this is so important to you?"

"I feel it is the key to my freedom, the answer to my question, or at least a doorway in the right direction."

"You have suffered greatly in your work," he said.

"Yes," I answered, surprised but relieved.

"This may end your suffering?"

"Yes, I think that is what Rory was telling me."

"It very well may, but you must try not to push too hard. It is good to be focused, but try also to remember to see more than what you look for. Where you are headed may not be where you need to go."

We began meeting every morning, sitting silent time together. I had forgotten what an excellent teacher Tolles was. He was thorough in his explanations and patient in his corrections. He conveyed a feeling of nonjudgment, helping me to learn in the way that best suited me. I was learning a series of postures designed to strengthen the body and assist in the activation. Tolles was uncannily sympathetic to what my body had been through from the venom, the areas that were weakened from it and why. I could not help but think he must work or somehow be involved with another Snake priestess. He knew things, intimate things, that only a Snake priestess would know.

"Your body has suffered greatly the ill effects of the venom," he said to me one day after we had been working together for a while. "You should know that until your body is stronger, we shall not begin practice toward activation. Your body in its present condition could not stand an awakening."

I was frustrated by this information, but continued to see him every morning, working diligently with the postures. I came to enjoy them and began to feel their beneficial effects upon my body. I felt myself standing taller, my back more supple. I felt strength increasing in my hips, my legs, my shoulders loosening. I became aware of weak places, my belly, my chest—how it had caved in upon itself.

With the practice came increased focus of mind; clarity of vision. As the time for my trance dance neared, I became agitated and distracted.

"Do not fear," Tolles said to me when I confessed my fear to him. "You shall see that our work will help even in these matters. Barbara has been hoping for a long time that you would discover us."

"Barbara?"

"Yes, she always suspected that a practice with the Serpent of Fire would help you."

"How is it that you know Barbara?"

Tolles' face had a look of uncertainty about it, a confusion I had never seen in it. "Because you ask, I shall tell you, though it places me in a rather uncomfortable position," he said, hesitating. "Barbara and I have been involved for some time now."

"Involved? You and Barbara? Do you mean . . ." I stopped myself and looked at him.

He nodded.

"I am not certain why Barbara has not told you, but as we both know Barbara, I know she has a good reason. Perhaps," he said after thinking for a minute, "you would be interested in hearing how we met?" He looked at me, his face a question.

I nodded in agreement to this.

"It was quite a while ago. When I think about it now, it surprises me. Our relationship has lasted a long time. I had only recently become a high priest when Barbara began to have her cycle of trance dances. It was I who was chosen to serve as her escort between temples for her dialogues about the Serpent of Fire.

"Of course, I was taken by her instantly, as everyone is, by her uncommon grace and beauty, her calm intelligence and deep wisdom, not to mention the way she handled those high priestesses and priests, who sometimes think they are more important than they are. Through all their continuous, repetitive questions and suspicious attitudes, she retained her dignity, never once letting them alter her.

"I began to feel nervous and uncomfortable around her. Her slightest move released to me the smell of her, leaving me dizzy and short of breath. I was making quite a fool of myself. It was very humiliating. I could find no place in which to anchor myself.

"To my benefit, Barbara was very bored by her life in the temple. Our walks became longer, extending into long stretches of the day. She did not seem to mind my frequent unannounced visits, though I knew myself to be overstepping my bounds.

"Until I saw what I had not been able to see before, until what I had been blind to became apparent, I could find no relief. Had I been less taken in, less engulfed by my attraction, I would have seen it. It had been there the whole time—the hearty laugh ending in a sudden stop, the long silences over certain subjects, the refusal to talk about the past. She was suffering greatly over the recent loss of a daughter, but, I had not noticed it until she told me.

"It is strange, and I do not understand it completely, but I am sure it was that—her pain—that finally grounded me. Being able finally to recognize her struggle allowed me to meet her as a person, and let her be a person as well.

"It has been very difficult for Barbara to have to watch you suffer. But this difficulty has proven to be, at the same time, a very healing thing. Since she was unable to help her daughter, being able to help and nurture you has seemed to her a gift—a second chance.

"Well, that is how it all began," he said, stretching his legs out from the crossed position they had been in beneath him. He folded his arms over them. "Barbara found out about you around the same time that I learned Danelle was my son. When we discovered that the two of you were connected, we laughed a good laugh at the coincidence. Now, however, we both know it is no coincidence."

* * *

"Why did you not tell me about Tolles?" I said, storming into the temple and disturbing everyone in it. "Why did I have to learn it from him? And who else knows? Danelle? Why must I always find things out in such a way?" I said, collapsing onto my knees beside her.

Barbara sat still, but her face had a look of surprise on it. I had, at last, caught her off guard.

"I knew this moment would come," she said, "and I knew you would be furious, which you have every right to be. I never did decide how I would handle it."

She fell silent, looking at me. "If I tell you that it was sheer instinct, not to tell you, that something within me just felt it would be better that you not know, would that satisfy you?"

I said nothing.

"I suppose not. Here it is, then," she said, straightening her spine and sitting up taller. "It was a difficult decision but, taking all circumstances into account, I felt it best that you not know so that you would feel completely supported by me, feel that you had all of my time and attention."

"When, in fact, I didn't."

"When, in fact, you did," she said.

"And Danelle, was he 'spared' this information?"

"Aureillia, Danelle has an extensive life outside the temple and he sees Tolles often. It was inevitable that he would find out before you."

"'Extensive life outside the temple.' It seems that eveyone does, except me."

"Poor dear, it is true. This too was part of the reason I did not tell you, to spare you from noticing all the things that you are missing."

I put my head on her lap and let a wave of sorrow pass through me. "I always wondered," I said, "whether or not you were involved with someone. I could find no reason in my mind that you would not be, but I have to say, I did not really want to know or I would have asked. I suppose the same instinct that kept me from asking kept you from telling. The way I need you so desperately made me hope, in fact, that you were not."

"Of course you need me and you need to feel completely supported. Tolles or no Tolles, you do have me and you are completely supported. If it were anyone other than Tolles, it would have been different, but the fact that it is he simply complicated things in certain ways." She stopped speaking and took some time to calm herself. "Are you all right?"

"Yes, quite," I said, lifting my head. "I feel somehow closer to you."

She smiled. "I am more of a person to you now?"

"Something like that," I said. "Isn't it remarkable, you and Tolles."

"I must say that you are handling this much better than Danelle did. He would not speak to me for weeks after he found out."

"What would ever make him act in such a way?"

"Poor Danelle, he felt I was taking everyone from him."

"Is that what he feels, that I have been 'taken from him?'"

"Of course he does, and he is right. You have been taken from him, but not by me."

"I do not understand why he cares for me so."

"'Cares for you,' that doesn't even come close," Barbara said.

I looked up at her. "What on earth do you mean?"

"When will you see who you are, Aureillia?"

"Who I am?"

 **CHAPTER 21**

The vision has a strange feel to it. I soar above, amid, and through a village. All I can hear, all I can feel, all I can sense, is wind—now blowing, now drifting, then swirling—circling in and within the rooms of these pale yellow, mud brick buildings, out through windows, down narrow alleyways. No people are present. There is no animal life. No human sounds. No animal voices. Only this place—this dry, empty place. Dust blows around with me in the wind, spinning, lifting within me. It is I. It is I who is blowing, swinging, weightless, floating—dropping, descending. I am wind. Wind am I, unable to control my direction—subject to the currents of air that push me about this village—into corners where, stuck, I remain until another current comes along and forces me out. I circle around a tall stone pillar that stands in the center of this village. I hover over the fields of rich, dark soil that lie on the slopes of the hill that this village sits upon. Larger hills rise, surrounding it, creating gentle, undulating curves of many colors.

"What a strange Snake," I said to Barbara when I awoke.

"You were so very calm during your vision," she said, "and you seem to be still."

"Yes," I said, sitting up. I could not get the feel of the vision to leave me. The feeling of being wind, but more than that—an eerie, haunted feeling. A feeling of familiarity, as though there were something I knew but could not remember. A nagging urge to hear something I could not hear.

"What is it?" Barbara asked, seeing my apprehension. "I really do not know. Something I know but cannot get to."

"What does that mean?"

"I don't know," I shook my head to try to make my mind leave it, but it would not. I could still feel it under there, working. "I cannot tell you because I do not know, but something is there—something I know but do not know, something I can hear but do not hear." I shrugged and threw my hands up in a gesture of surrender.

Barbara looked at me with concern but had nothing to say. She looked thin and pale. I had not noticed it before. "You look ill," I said, "are you quite all right?"

"Ill?" she said. "No, not ill."

I returned to Tolles feeling much more energetic than I had thought I would. I was calmer about wanting to rush into the learning, feeling for the first time that perhaps I did not want to get where I was going any faster than I was being led.

I thought a great deal about the Serpent of Fire. I wondered how many people around me were engaged in the active uncoiling of Her power within them. I wondered whether there was any way to know who had. I remembered Metha telling me so long ago about the serpent who longs to speak to women as they bleed. "So it is that women go to the red grotto to better hear Her," Metha had said.

"Yes," Tolles said, when I asked him. "It is true that as a woman bleeds the Serpent of Fire often becomes activated. I wish I were permitted to enter the red grotto. I'm sure it is quite an incredible place."

"So it is," I said to him. "I believe it is one of the most beautiful places on our island."

"You misunderstand my meaning," he said. "It is not the place to which I refer, but rather the power felt in the presence of many activated serpents."

I was sure I did not understand, but held my tongue from the desire for an explanation.

Danelle was very involved in working on a sculpture he had been asked to create for the entryway to the main court. He had been asked to display the Goddess in her tree spirit form, using wood.

Miniatures were still his specialty and he rarely worked with wood, but the request was such an honor that he took it on with gratitude and great seriousness. The entryway to the main court was a small, high-ceilinged, corridorlike room that separated the court from the outside world. Everyone who used the main entrance passed through this entryway. The doors leading into the court and going outside were quite wide and, when open, allowed plenty of light in. The sculpture was to hang above the doorway that led into the court. Danelle had been asked to make her large enough to fill the entire wall above this doorway.

He insisted on working on Her in the entryway. He said he wanted to create Her where She would be, making Her one with the room and the Center building around Her. "How can I sculpt Her face without seeing what Her eyes will be seeing?" he said, forcing them to shut down the entryway until She was complete.

Frequently, after my lessons with Tolles, I would go to the main entry to watch him work. It was grand to finally be able to observe his method. I was surprised by how involved the muscles on his back were in the work, especially the fine detail work. I looked forward to the time when he became hot enough to remove his shirt so that I could watch the small movements between and around his shoulder blades.

He rarely spoke to me so involved was he in the work. And though I sometimes stood behind him for long periods of time, even speaking softly with his apprentice, who was building the stand that would hold Her, some evenings he would act surprised that I had been there that day.

He thought about Her constantly, drifting off in the middle of a conversation, interrupting at other times to ask questions about Her, working through the night, falling asleep beside Her. His intensity and focus were astounding. I realized he must be like this with all his work, but I had not been able to witness it until now.

*   *   *

In trance, I am wind again, drifting through the same village, in which, this time, the people who live here are present. The place is so very different with people. It is alive and full of different energies. There is less room for me to move about in. I get caught in more places, bumping against all this dense, heavy matter. I create less sound.

People in this village occupy themselves in the usual ways: baking breads, working metal upon a fire, carrying water, tending to children. There is a large market now, spread in a circle around the pillar, where various wares have been brought for trading. Upon the tables lie woven items, fish, and baskets. I am stuck circling above this for a while until I am pushed suddenly by a stronger wind from behind me toward the enclave of houses. I am forced inside a house and down some steps that lead to another corner, which opens into a circling stairway dropping deep, deeper. I swirl down it, caught upon air, descending, descending, landing in caves of rooms—rooms of caves deep underground—passing through narrow passageways dug into this cool, moist rock, on and on through this massive underground chamber, almost as large as the village that sits above it, concealing it. The stairs turn into an overhang, which wraps around all sides of a large domed room. Rising up from below are the whispering voices of women. Over the overhang I drift, slowly falling down, down, down into this room where, as I get closer to the floor, I see women sitting—praying. This is a shrine. A central shrine. The women kneel toward a bench type altar beside which stands another pillar, mirroring the one I have seen in the center of the aboveground village. Several offerings are set upon the bench, honey cakes and shaped breads, clay vessels. The women's heads are covered in cloth that drapes down and over their shoulders. I cannot see any of their faces, as I am caught circling among and between them. I get stuck near two of them who are kneeling very close to each other. They turn their heads toward me at the exact same time, in the exact same way, as though they see me. Outside my head I hear my own voice speaking. Again it is dull and muted. I feel myself moving. I feel Barbara's hand upon mine, trying to calm me, but there is no calming me. I continue saying it, over and over, repeating, "It is I! It is I! It is us!" So shocked am I at the sight of Barbara's and my faces looking at me from within those shawls.

I am shaken when I awake. Such a strange feeling visits me. I only lie there looking up at the ceiling. An emptiness fills me. A void. Barbara's face looking down at me makes me shiver in memory of what I have just seen.

"Aureillia, are you all right?"

"Oh my," I say, closing my eyes and covering them with my arm, "oh my."

Throughout the moon, the vision haunted me. It sat within my vision. It was there when I closed my eyes. When they were open, the feeling was there, pressing at me, surging. I was utterly confused. I could not concentrate in meditation. I kept thinking about something Rory had said, that she and Zula had known each other before. Those words had meant nothing to me then—but how they resonated within me now.

"Did you know that eagles have three eyelids?" Barbara asked. We were sitting up on a cliff, a watchpoint for a huge funnel shaped eagle's nest in a tree below it. We had been sitting here often of late. An eagle pair were busily involved in the rebuilding of their nest, which, until now, had been abandoned and empty. They worked on it diligently, adding another few inches to the top of it, preparing together for the season's offspring.

"Three eyelids?" I responded. "I did not know that."

"Yes. It is most intriguing," she said, keeping her eye on the nest below us. "The third and innermost one actually moves horizontally across their eye. It is used most often in flight to keep their eyes clear and clean as they soar. And they can soar. Eagles can really soar. Imagine not only being able to soar, but also to have the ability to maintain clear vision while you soar. That is a rare gift indeed."

"Barbara," I said, "do you believe that you and I were supposed to work together, that it was somehow meant to be?"

"Of course," she said without hesitation.

"Why?"

"I do not know why. I only know that one of my purposes is to help you attain wisdom from the Snakes. What about you?" she said, looking at me. "Do you feel that we were meant to work together?"

"Of course I feel that way, only I do not know why I feel that way. You see, I want to understand why I feel that way."

"Her most important teachings do not always manifest themselves in words," Barbara said. She stopped watching the eagles and turned to me. "From us the Goddess requires great trust. The trust that is hardest to give: trusting in that which we cannot see. That within you which has no name, Aureillia. That which has no words, no shape, yet knows all—that is Her residing within you. It is through trusting in this that we become free."

"I have underestimated your wisdom," I said.

"You have underestimated your own wisdom, Aureillia," she said. "Trust. Let it flow through you."

* * *

I am wind, spreading myself through what they call the Hills of Judah. I circle around the aboveground village. I circle around the pillar of the Goddess which has been broken, shattered into pieces. She lies crushed, Her mutilated pieces lying in sharp shards around Her. The axe that ruined Her lies still beside Her. People walk over Her, some even walk upon Her, their careless feet breaking Her into still more pieces. I have never seen such a thing. I have seen people destroy sacred places before they leave them unattended, or before rebuilding them. I have seen priestesses break sculptures of Her to remove their power when they are no longer useful, lest they fall into the wrong hands, but the pieces are always carefully stored away. It is done with ever so much respect and adoration. To see something like this, Her likeness lying smashed and openly broken, is an affront to my eyes. I settle down upon the ground next to Her.

"Pillar," I say, "Oh, poor pillar. What has happened to you?"

"These people," She says, sorrow permeating her voice, "these people will suffer for me. The man who took his axe to me only went to gather help. He will return shortly to destroy the entire village."

"But why?"

"I am forbidden."

"Forbidden? How can the Goddess be forbidden? You are the very air itself."

"You shall see. It is forbidden."

I am pushed away from the pillar. Swirling again within the underground chambers, I arrive at a hidden shrine where five women sit praying. Among them are Barbara and Aureillia. Barbara leads the prayer. Upon the altar are sculptures of the Goddess entwined with snakes. They remember. They remember Minoa. They remember each other. I can tell from the air that stands between them as I travel through it; tight, familiar, unified. When the ritual is complete, Barbara and Aureillia stay behind and hide the sculptures in a hidden door behind the altar. They whisper to each other and exchange gentle touch. There is worry. Barbara looks around the room. She looks at me. She can feel me. She hugs Aureillia close to her.

# CHAPTER 22

Danelle had been putting curls of bronze hair on the sculpture. She was almost complete. He had carved her from the wood of a cedar tree. Her scent—strong and mossy, present everywhere within this entryway—urged one toward Her, making one aware, even when not looking up, of the presence of this powerful, deep, dark tree woman.

We stood together, looking up at her. A serpent uncoiled from deep within her strong brown and curving body—traveling up the length of her belly, between her breasts, up over her throat and head, upon which it sprouted into many red serpent locks of hair. The long bronze shavings he had used for hair hung down around her, casting an illuminating light upon her body.

"She is supreme," I said in awe.

"Yes," he agreed, "I am quite pleased."

Much to Danelle's dismay, people had not only continued calling his signature stones "amulets," but were now calling them "amulets of the oracle."

"I wish they would not call them that," he said one night when I found him, clearly distressed, at our meeting place.

"But why?" I said, kneeling close beside him. "Why does it bother you so?"

"Because it gives me too much power. It implies that I know more than they—calling me an oracle? It's absurd."

"Apparently they do not agree."

"But don't you see, Aureillia," he said, looking at me, his eyebrows close together, arms folded upon his upraised knees, "by calling me an oracle, they place their own power outside themselves. They act as though I know things they do not. But they do know them. They only use me to tell them things they already know."

"That is true. I see it more as an affirmation for them—a welcome and surprising agreement of what they suspect most deeply within themselves."

"Can you not see the danger in that?"

"Danelle, why can't you see what everyone else knows instinctively? In you this power can be trusted. It is clear to all that you will use it only in the most responsible and thoughtful manner."

"That is a very large expectation," he said.

"You seem to be up to it."

"But what if I am not? What if I am no longer able to fulfill all these wishes and requests? What if I wake up one day and it is gone or I don't want to do it anymore?"

"Then you will do something else. Then it will be time to move on. Do not let it own you."

"Danelle," I said to him now, turning away from the sculpture and toward him. "You have activated your serpent, haven't you?"

"Yes," he said, but he was looking at the sculpture, his eyes deeply exploring her.

I watched him with eyes that were seeing him in a new way: how he stood there, straight and tall, hands on his hips, face forward. How his body was at once relaxed and attentive, how his strong brown legs bent slightly at the knees, firm yet flexible.

The heat rose within me, from deep below, surging upward, filling my chest and head. I put my hands up to my face to cool my burning cheeks.

"What?" he said, turning himself toward me.

"You," I said, shaking my head. "You."

* * *

"Barbara," I said one night as we took our evening walk, "I must ask you a question."

"Does it pertain to the visions?"

"Yes, it does. I won't tell you the vision. I only need direction about a certain issue. I do not know whom else to ask."

She thought about it for some time. "It is difficult for me to know whether or not I should let you ask the question," she said finally, "because I do not know what the question is." She laughed a loud, hearty laugh at what she had heard herself say.

"Yes, I understand," I said. "You could refuse to answer it after I have asked it, if you so please."

"Does it bother you terribly?"

"Mercilessly."

"Ask it, then."

"Do you believe there are other lives, in other times and places, that we live?"

She looked at me for a time, deep in thought. "I will not tell you my beliefs on this matter," she said, "because I have too great an influence upon you. But I will tell you that for a question of this sort, one must seek guidance from a priestess in the temple of the Butterfly."

"The Butterfly," I said. "Of course."

Why had I not thought about it on my own? I entered the temple of the Butterfly the next day. Through those open doors of light and air where years earlier I had come in search of assistance, I now returned.

But this time, instead of staying in the airy, winged upper part of the temple, I was led back in and through the silk corridors down steps into the lower rooms. Here it was very dark and cavelike.

"There are many stages for the butterfly," the priestess that I followed commented when she recognized my surprise. "It is only through entering the darkness of the cocoon that transformation may begin, and that, though unknown to the caterpillar, is always a deliberate act."

"Deliberate?" I said.

"Always."

She led me into the lower temple and presented me to a woman with many annums to her, sitting in a chair. Though this usually signaled the inability to sit any longer on the floor, her body seemed robust and strong. Her face, though very wrinkled, was round and smiling. She had a broad, spreading nose, and her eyes, though buried deep beneath grey clouds, sparkled with alertness.

"I have always had a fondness for Snake priestesses," she said, extending her hands to me. "They are always the feisty ones." She took my hands into hers with a firmness I had not expected. Her hands, strong and awake, held mine confidently, pulling me in closer. "Are you quite well, my dear?"

"I wish to be," I said.

"And so you shall," she said. "I can tell you now, you shall."

I looked at her hopefully.

"Eventually," she added, shaking my hands up and down within hers. "Eventually. Come, tell me what it is that brings you to me today."

I presented her with my question.

She sat thinking for a long time, sucking in her bottom lip. "I am sure the answer to your question has to be yes," she said. "Here, in the temple of the Butterfly, we strongly believe that endings are merely doorways, beginnings. Our preachings center themselves on the belief in departure from the earth plane as a form of transformation—a change to something new, different. We do not necessarily believe that this means change into the form of another person in another time and place, but it most certainly could. Indeed, there are those who believe it. Many have wondered over this question of yours," she said. "Please, when you are able to divulge more information, return to us. Your knowledge would be most valuable."

"There is one more thing," I said. "Do you have any insight as to why someone would be shown a portion of another lifetime?"

"Lessons," she said, nodding her head and sucking her bottom lip in again. "It is about lessons. There are lessons to be learned." Her eyes peered at me so intensely that, for a moment, I saw the younger person she had been. She gripped my right hand. "Always look for the lesson," she said.

I had not realized the gift Danelle had given me until I returned to my practice. Though we had been working toward activation for some time, my body having attained the necessary physical strength, I had not been successful. The practice toward activation involved extended periods of silent time, growing gradually longer. "Become aware of the serpent resting coiled at the base of your spine," Tolles would say when it became clear I had entered the mystical state. I had been dropping my focus, and resting there, but was unable to make anything happen. I had not been able to get a conceptual idea of this serpent until now.

I closed my eyes and saw Danelle's sculpture. I focused on the image of Her, the bronze, red serpent uncoiling within her, releasing divine energy up through her. This image that he had created planted itself within me, making what I had not been able to visualize appear before me in dimensional form.

I became aware of a movement, a tiny tongue licking the bone at the base of my spine, spreading heat out to the whole of the bottom part of my body, my hips and around to my back, warm and tingly, like hot oil flowing within me. She uncoiled herself slowly, up my spine. I felt her pass through each individual bone along my back, sending penetrating heat out to the other parts of my body, continuing upward until she reached my head, where she exploded into roundness, filling my skull. As she passed out the opening at the top of my head, her two ends stretched away from each other, lengthening, radiating more power.

I looked at Tolles. There was a shocking red serpent of light stretching up from the base of his spine and out the top of his head, pulsing and flickering.

"What is it?" he asked.

"I can see you," I said.

"Close your eyes that you may focus upon the feeling," he said.

I closed my eyes. He was right. I had forgotten my own serpent by looking at his. The heat was everywhere within me, spreading outside the physical limits of my body. I floated upon its warmth, cradled in compassion.

Tolles was beaming. "Only awakened serpents can see other serpents," he said, "but you must know that even most awakened serpents cannot see other serpents. It is a rare gift. I am not surprised that you possess it, however. Indeed, you have an exceptional gift of vision."

I looked at Tolles. Such an odd feeling overcame me. It had been such a long time since I had thought of my abilities as a gift. I had quite forgotten that what I was doing I was doing because of a gift I had been given.

I continued to see the serpent lights within people. It was utter delight. The whole island was aflicker. Everywhere I went I saw them, some curled and dormant, some weak, some halfway uncoiled, but many full grown and floating, swimming, swaying freely within the person who possessed them. Most were red, but now and then there would appear different colors. I was astonished by vibrant greens, pinks and purples. I took a walk to the red grotto.

Inside the cool, dark cavern was a sight of pulsing lights so beautiful I was sorry that Tolles would never experience it. Then I sought out Danelle.

I found him on the crest of a hill, on a path leading into one of the forests surrounding Knossos.

"What is it?" he asked, as I approached him.

I stood back in awe of him: a bright red serpent pulsed thick and strong within him, shining a red sheen upon his skin, around his body, off the ends of his hair. "You are so beautiful, Danelle," I said.

"What are you talking about?"

"I can see you. I can see you! You are magnificent!"

"You can see it? You can see the serpent?"

"Yes."

"What does it look like?"

"It is red, the red of a freshly bloomed poppy. It pulses. It pulses and surges within you. It carries light. It shines a red glow around you."

He put his arms around me. "I cannot see it," he said. "Maybe you lag behind, but you always manage to outdo me." He leaned in to kiss me. Red flames leapt from his mouth toward me.

I backed away.

"What is it?"

"It is frightening."

"Close your eyes."

"Of course," I said. I closed my eyes and opened my mouth. I could feel the flames entering me even before his lips were upon mine. "Can you feel it?" I asked.

"It is amazing," he said.

We kissed until the heat from him penetrated the back of my throat, where I felt it meeting my own serpent, which was gold. They mixed together, flowing up and down my spine. I felt his new, different energy penetrating, stimulating, entering all parts of my body. The heat within me increased until I was close to burning.

"Danelle," I said. I wanted to ask him if he was feeling what I was feeling, but when I opened my eyes I was stunned by the serpent that was streaming between us. Our serpents were combined into a golden red color. It flowed like running water between us, into us, through us, in a circular motion. I reached my hand out to touch it.

"Magic," I said.

We looked into each other's eyes until our eyes were one. No words came, but I heard him. I heard everything that he said.

CHAPTER 23

Barbara's serpent swam within her as she walked in front of me to my trance dance, a deep, elegant purple glow about her.

I was distracted in my dance, allowing the snake to give me a nasty bite on the back of my ankle.

"Oh, no," I heard myself say, as I dropped clumsily to the floor.

Back in the village I am wind whipping around fiercely. I am a whirlwind circling above the pillar, who still lies on the ground, broken.

"Why have they not repaired you?" I ask.

There is no response.

"Pillar," I say, "why is it that they have not yet repaired you?"

"The Goddess is murdered," she says in a whisper, as though waking from slumber. Then once again, a little louder this time, "The Goddess is murdered."

"Murdered? That is not possible."

"Watch and see watch and see
What they have done to me
They do to the image of me."

Her voice becomes louder and louder as she repeats her chant into the desolate air around her.

"Watch and see watch and see
What they have done to me"

The chanting becomes shrill shrieking. I am trying to bring my hands to my ears. I want it to stop. I do not want to hear her, but I am wind, only to be blown here and there by forces outside of myself.

I am pushed by so many hooves galloping hurriedly toward us. I am caught within and among the many moving legs of a group of horses, pushed into the dust they carry with them, forced upward through the tight air between their strong, pulsing, pungent bodies. I am forced into the faces of the darkly dressed men who sit upon them, axes and swords mere extensions of their hands.

"Oh, no," I hear myself moaning. "Pillar was right."

Widespread panic overtakes the village as people run and scream, pushing each other in terror. Yet in the middle of all this chaos, I am presented with a most splendid sight. These people, this village, is full of serpent lights. They swirl red, pink, orange, purple within these Goddess loving people as they flee—as they run. I am blowing toward their houses, caught within the crowd of people fleeing into the underground chambers, pushing and crowding into doorways, down stairs. I am released through the doorway of the hidden shrine of the Snake Goddess where I find Barbara behind the altar breaking the heads and arms off the sculptures to remove their power in proper ritual manner. She wraps the pieces together in purple silk and returns them to their hiding place. Her movements are quick and tense. Her hands shake in fear. Aureillia appears in the doorway.

"Hurry," she cries to Barbara, her brown eyes large.

"They're coming. Many of them."

An arm snatches her from behind. She pulls away from it and runs down the stairs. I am stuck in the wind of the man who chases her. He grabs the end of her shawl. She lets it go, sending him toppling backward, exposing her back, her white, sleeveless dress. She flees down more stairs, reaching the balcony overhang above the central shrine. He is again behind her. He raises his axe above her. She turns to see him. Horror fills her face before she turns back around, hands covering her face as his axe enters bluntly the skin of her back, slicing into the space between her shoulder blades over and over again. Her white dress turns a deep, soaking red. She falters. She stumbles. He pushes her gently forward so that she topples over the balcony, spinning gracefully through the air in twirling circles before landing on the shrine floor on top of others who have fallen before her. Her eyes stare up at me as I swirl above her—the open eyes of death. Her serpent light flickers, flickers, flickers, before it goes out.

I am stuck circling slowly in the thick air of this shrine filled with fresh, wet death. The men have left. All is quiet. I fear I shall never be released from the sight that haunts me from below.

Barbara appears at the overhang. Her pained gasp fills the chamber when she sees Aureillia looking up at her. She descends the stairs quickly, moving bodies out of the way to get to her. She throws herself on top of Aureillia, releasing desperate sobs that echo off the walls. Her serpent light, so purple and bright until now, begins to fade, to lose color, to flicker, until it descends downward swiftly, landing in a tight coil at the bottom of her spine. There it slowly spins, its small light only an ember from what was once a tall, roaring fire. She closes Aureillia's eyelids tenderly with her fingers. She stands up, stooped, and begins to walk away. She has lost her vital light, her power.

Power.

"Power," I hear myself saying. "Power. Power."

When I woke up I was still chanting it. I was so afraid to forget. "Power. Power," I repeated.

"Aureillia, Aureillia, it's me. Look at me."

I opened my eyes to see Barbara leaning over me.

I took her hand and grasped fiercely. "I know what it is about," I said. "I know why. Power, Barbara, it's about power. Stealing power."

"Power?" she said, grasping my hand. "Whose power? What power?"

"Our power. Women's power. Hypia is right—it's about stealing women's power." She looked at me, her face at once a question and a recognition, but then it turned into a smile as she said, "Aureillia, do you know what this means? You're finished. You have finished your cycle of trance dances. You are free," she said, taking me into her arms and smothering me with kisses. "You are free!"

CHAPTER 24

Though I was relieved to be finished with my trance dances, relieved in the knowing that this recovery from the venom would be my last, relieved in having received an answer to the question that had disturbed me for so long, I was not filled with happiness as I had always imagined I would be.

The last vision had left me ill with worry and despair. The pillar's shrill chanting had become a part of me; her song sang within me, repeating over and over without end.

I had lost my serpent and with it, the ability to see serpent lights. But the thing that filled me with pain and sorrow, that drove me to desperation and nighttime wanderings, the thing that I absolutely could not tolerate, was the fact that Barbara was waning.

She had taken to bed a few days after my last trance dance and had not been able to get herself out. The herbalist met me in the corridor and told me it would not be long.

I went outside and ran and ran until I reached a place far, far away from the Center, where I buried myself in the deep grasses and screamed the scream that was inside me so that no one else need suffer from it. Then I went to see her.

She lay under a blanket woven of pink lambswool. Her face was drawn and thin. Dark circles surrounded her eyes. I sat on the edge of the bed beside her.

"It seems I will not last very much longer, Aureillia," she said, looking at me. "I am so sorry to not be able to help you complete your prophecy."

"Maybe they are wrong. Maybe you shall become better," I said hopefully, knowing I was being foolish.

Barbara smiled. "Yes, maybe," she said. "To be honest, I am surprised I made it through the cycle of trance dances. For a while I did not think that I would." She straightened the fold of her blanket under her arms, stretching her two hands across the length of it repetitively before patting it and then folding her hands together upon it. She looked away from me.

"You poor thing," I said. "Have you been waiting for me?"

"I thought you would never finish," she laughed. I laughed too, but it was a laugh full of pain and it ended quickly. This pain, it was physical. Every part of my body throbbed with the ache of it.

She began to straighten the fold of the blanket again, though it needed no straightening. I enfolded her hands with mine. She squeezed them tight.

"It is good," she said, "for a woman of the venom to go in this way—quickly. You will wish the same for yourself when the time comes."

There was so much I wanted to tell her, yet I could think of nothing to say. Sobs from deep under my ribs surged up within me. My chest heaved. I gasped for air. "Oh, Barbara," I said, placing my head upon her chest.

Her hands caressed my hair. "I am so lucky to have been your mentor," she said. "You have done a good thing, Aureillia." She lifted my face toward hers. A fierceness and power shone out from it. "You will find goodness in what you have discovered. Do not devalue the work we have done."

On the third day, the priestesses of the Butterfly prepared to return her. I dressed myself in ritual attire in her honor. It was the last time we would wear our Snake priestess dresses together. I joined the procession with the other Snake priestesses as it left the Center, winding toward the Cave of Return; escorting her back to the Goddess.

The procession was long with people stretching for a great distance along the path of return. The great bronze labrys, as wide as a tree is tall, led the way. It was carried by three priestesses of the Butterfly supporting it from three large wooden posts.

Behind the labrys, other priestesses of the Butterfly carried Barbara, lying upon the platform in Snake priestess attire, the crown of golden snakes upon her auburn hair.

The Cave of Return is set deep inside Her hill. Facing to the east, the priestesses return Barbara. The huge bronze labrys is placed within its holder outside the cave. The priestesses lead us in chant.

The wind pushes against the labrys which shakes and shimmers. All at once the sun strikes it with such ferocity that the crowd drops to its knees in awe and shock at the blinding light shining off it. I remain standing, looking into that light that is so bright I can feel it tearing at the browns of my eyes, as She swallows Barbara, purring, wrapping Her earth self happily around her.

Something makes me look to my right. It is Danelle. He is standing up in the midst of the crowd of kneeling people. He is looking at me.

# CHAPTER 25

I clanged around the temple, empty yet noisy. There was no place for me there without Barbara. I struggled with my prophecy, working on it constantly, spread out upon the temple floor. I saw no one, keeping to the temple except for meals, where I sat alone at the table farthest removed from others.

With Barbara gone, Danelle dared not enter the temple. Though I often saw him standing outside the door for long periods of time, I did not go to him.

Tolles came to me in the temple one day as I scribbled angrily at my prophecy. Beneath me I hoarded Barbara's pillow; in my hand I held tightly the braided lock of her hair that she had given me.

"Come back to your practice, Aureillia," he implored. "You must find peace."

I did not answer him, but continued scratching into the clay.

"Aureillia, there is much conflict within you. Let me help you. I can help you through this."

"No," I said, looking up at him. I knew how I looked, so the shock in his face did not bother me. I had not slept since Barbara's departure. "I will not return. I will not be deceived again. To be granted a gift only to understand a horror," I said to him, my voice loud and furious. "To have it taken away in the most vile way. My work is finished. She has no use for me any longer."

"Such bitterness will serve you no purpose, Aureillia."

"Such bitterness serves my every purpose," I said, retuning to my work, rubbing the fingers of my left hand upon the braid as I wrote with the other.

He remained standing above me for a while before he turned and walked away.

Behind the wooden Snake Goddess I stand; She with the enlarged ears. She who stares in trance. The crown of golden snakes adorns my head, the armbands circle my arms.

The court is filled with people waiting, anxious. They have all heard tell that the time has come, the prophetess of darkness will speak. I close my eyes as She rolls around the court floor. The words I have practiced over and over pour loudly out of me, passing through the hole of her wooden mouth. Echoing through the court, they say:

> *"In a world where the Goddess is murdered*
> *These things shall come to pass*
> *In ceremonies of death*
> *The flesh of live women will burn*
> *The skies to our north*
> *To thick black smoke will turn*
> *The power of healing forgotten*
> *Blood flows*
> *When in a woman*
> *It should not flow*
> *Mutilation!*
> *Knives knowing places*
> *A knife should never know*
> *The power of pleasure forbidden*
> *Women!*
> *To steal your power*
> *This violence upon you they shower*
> *She shall be shattered*
> *Her images smashed and battered*
> *There She lies in many pieces*
> *As worshipping of Her ceases*
> *Fear not, Minoans*
> *Your love of the Goddess is clear*
> *Remember that*
> *Only in a world where the Goddess is murdered*
> *Shall these things come to pass"*

I turned around within the wooden sculpture. Eyes focused on the closest exit, I walked directly toward it.

Outside the rains pounded down hard and deliberate. I walked through them, pounding back. I was not walking toward anything; I was walking away from all.

"Aureillia!" Danelle's voice called from behind me. I continued walking.

"Aureillia, stop!" he cried.

I stopped. He caught up to me. His breathing was heavy from the distance he had run. His hair and clothing were drenched.

He grabbed my arm into his two hands firmly, almost harshly, as though grasping for something he knew he had already lost.

"It is over now. You can start new. Don't go, Aureillia. Please don't leave me."

"Forgive me," I said, pulling at my arm.

He held firm. "No. I do not forgive you," he said. "I will not forgive you. Do not go."

"Try to find a way to forgive me," I said, pulling my arm free with more force than I knew I possessed.

He fell to his knees, sobbing.

I turned and walked away from him.

PART III

# CHAPTER 26

It was a relief to stumble at last upon the cave. For days I had walked, the rains fell—cooling me through to the juices. My legs walked on, carrying me farther and farther. They stopped only to rest under trees whose large, drooping branches offered shelter.

I did not see the cave until I fell forward into it.

It was dark and raining. I had been fumbling along with outstretched arms for some time, when I toppled suddenly into it. I searched around in the darkness for some pieces of dry wood, which I gathered into a pile near the entryway. After repeated efforts, I was unable to bring them to flame and so collapsed into sleep.

In the morning, I was surprised to wake up to an overwhelming view of a meeting of sea and sky. The cave sat up on a hill that looked down upon a rounded cove. The cove was surrounded by craggy rocks reaching into tall cliffs around it. The waters were so still within this hidden cove that it seemed to be an illusion. I would not let myself believe it completely until I had walked down to the small sandy beach and put my hands into the wetness.

The cave had a high, rounded ceiling. The floor was smooth, almost polished. One could easily see that the sea had once made Her home within it. She was everywhere upon it in deposits of Her creatures; imprints of their tiny bones. The floor sloped down toward the back of the cave.

In the day's light, I was able to gather up more dry wood and some brush, which I brought to flame inside the cave. I sat in the opening, watching. In the distance I could see the sails of boats passing by, reflecting against the wind. None came near. Within the cove waters were many tall rocks reaching up and out of the waters. They must have extended out into deeper waters as well, making it unsafe for boats.

For three days and three nights, I stayed there alone. During the days, I wandered about, getting to know the area. On the second day, I discovered a steep path to the right of the cave which led into a densely wooded area. This was the way I must have entered this place. I was able to forage, digging up roots and eating berries. My sleep was infrequent and uncomfortable. I woke up many times, frightened, having revisited the places of my visions in dreamtime. I would sit awake inside the dark coldness of the cave—the fire having gone out—and think about Barbara. My body swelled with the loss of her. Her face as I had last seen it, pale and drawn, hung stubbornly within my inner vision.

I sat there night after night, remembering her; seeing her, wanting desperately to talk to her. One moment I would feel sad, the next angry and cheated, the next, lonely. So many different feelings were running through me, tugging me in different directions. I was furious that it was the venom that had taken her—the venom she had taken from me. I wished over and over that she had not done that. I imagined scenes of myself not allowing her to do it, saying no. I was desperate over the fact that I had not stopped her. *How could I have let her do that? Oh, why did I let her do that?* I asked myself over and over again.

On the third night, as I sat in the opening of the cave watching the sun's slow and brilliant descent, I heard a rustling—the sound of a large sail catching the wind. In the distance I saw something dark and mysterious flying toward me. It became larger and larger as it got closer. The sound was the wind upon its outstretched wings.

This is too large to be an owl, I thought to myself, backing into the cave.

She came to land in the entryway. A magnificent, winged woman.

Long, thick, black hair. Strong dark eyebrows. Bright green eyes. Beaked nose above small, pink mouth. Skin of copper-red.

She wore no clothing, exposing Her breasts between two enormous feathered wings, whose span filled the opening of the cave. She had hairy legs and the clawed feet of an owl.

Moss and cedar, her fragrance permeated the dense air of the cave. I stared at her, backing away until I reached the wall behind me and could go no farther.

"Who are you?" I asked.

"I am Lilith," she said "Keeper of secrets." She lowered her wings and approached me, looming very tall above me. "I have come that you may give me yours."

"From where? From where have you come?"

"From the future, the past and the now," she said.

I tried to back away farther, but there was nowhere to go. Lilith turned and walked toward the fire. She sat herself down in front of it, her feathered back to me. "I know," she said to the fire, "the form is difficult at first."

I stood, looking at her back, how the feathers—which from a distance had looked black and grey but were actually black and brown with flecks of white—hung around her like a shawl.

"You will soon become cold in that corner," she said. "Come, sit across the fire from me."

I walked to a place directly across from her, the fire between us, and sat down.

"Your sleep needs guarding," she said, poking at the fire with a large stick, bringing up sparks. "For this purpose I have come."

I sat up, watching her through the fire until I could not sit up any more and let myself lie down and then, finally, surrender to slumber. My sleep was again fitful, waking me. Everytime I awoke I would see her, sitting in the same place, awake, watching me, the fire blazing high between us.

In the morning, as the sun rose, she left—flying away, her wide wings spanning the horizon. At sun's setting she returned, clutching food within her clawed feet.

All through the nights to follow she would sit across the fire from me. When my dreams woke me, I would sit up and stare into the red flames she kept burning tall. No words passed between us. Though the form I still found difficult, her dark, silent presence offered me comfort.

One night I awoke in panic, gasping for breath. I tried to rid myself of the horrors of my last vision, which had replayed inside my dreamtime. I shook my head and covered my eyes. I stood up and paced and circled on my side of the fire.

"Tell it all to me," Lilith said, breaking the silence between us. "Tell me all your secrets. I shall hold them for you that you may live a human life."

So it was that I began to tell Lilith my secrets. Each night, after I had eaten, I would sit across the fire from her and tell a story. I started with the first vision, then moved on from there, closing my eyes to better remember. I could feel how the words that left me reached her differently—how the passage through the fire changed them, how they arrived to her polished—burnt clean.

At first I was hesitant, not wanting to let them go, uneasy with their form after they left me. As we continued to work, however, the sense of relief became larger than that part of me that longed to cling. I began to look forward to my nighttime storytelling, yearning to reveal myself further; shed another layer.

I could feel how Lilith absorbed them, how she was able to hold them within herself without becoming altered by them. Each time I would complete a cycle, she would nod her head and say, "This too, shall come to pass."

"Where do you go," I asked her finally one night, "when you leave here?"

"My home is in the Red Sea," she said. "I go to attend to the many matters of my children."

"Children? Have you many children?"

"All who discover the murder of the Goddess are my children. I come to assist them through this most difficult discovery. You, Aureillia, are my child."

"Are there many like me?"

"Many, and yet, too few. There is much work to be done."

"Work?"

"Yes. Work."

"What kind of work?"

"What is broken may be repaired," Lilith said, then low, almost in a chant, "Gather Her many pieces. Make Her whole."

"'Gather her many pieces'," I repeated. "Not gone forever?"

"Nothing gone forever."

"Of course," I said, looking at her. A current of feeling filled my being. It was so strong and possessing, I had to stand up to contain it. I stood up. I let it radiate through me. I gasped in the joy of it; the feeling of hope.

"But how?" I asked.

Lilith looked up at me with a half smile. "Yes," she said, tilting her head to one side. "How?"

# CHAPTER 27

After a time at the cove, something wonderful happened. I began to bleed again. Once again, the warming liquid flowed within me, through me, and out of me, together with the rhythm of the moon. I luxuriated in the silky ebb and flow of the tides within me, in the downpour of the warm, cleansing liquid, the dependable and continuous cycle of building slowly toward eventual release.

I resumed my daily practice of sitting silent time, focusing. Slowly, my concentration increased and I began to have visions. Strange, solemn, still visions of women, singular women. Each time a different woman, appeared before me—a many colored rainbow of women—facing me but not seeing me. One wore a great deal of clothing and was hunched inside a great fluffy chair that threatened to encompass her. One stood tall, seemed to beam hostility, arms crossed in front of herself. One carried a heavy pack on her back, shoulders bending under the weight of it.

I had not regained my ability to see the serpent, and I doubted I would. I truly believed that I had only been given the opportunity to better understand my visions. I had come to accept this. I had wanted to understand. I had asked for assistance and I had received it.

Even so, I worked again toward awakening the serpent within, knowing that my physical body was again weakened and it would take some time.

But these women—these odd, ethereal, women, who appeared before me. How they intrigued and puzzled me, again pulling me toward becoming a question.

"What? What are you trying to say to me?" I would say, irritated by their persistent presence, but they would simply keep looking at me, in them nothing changing. It was clear that they were saying what they had to say; it was I who was not hearing them.

Since I could not get any understanding of what they were about, they began to annoy me. I only wanted to regain my focus, to work on my silent time, and these women were constantly interrupting me. I could not get around them or get rid of them and I could not make any sense of them. I was unable to move forward in my practice.

I found a rock in the water that I could sit upon, immersing my lower body in the waters while I practiced. I thought the water could help me clear away these images to better focus my mind. But, even submerged in water, they continued to appear, floating upon the clear surface, the same women, over and over, repeating themselves as flashes through my inner vision.

I trudged, frustrated, through the wooded forest. "Why will they not leave me alone? I wish to be left alone," I muttered to myself. But I knew, I knew as I had so many times before, that it was my responsibility to understand—mine and mine alone.

"But I am so very tired," I said to the air, the cool morning moisture making a cloud out of my breath.

The next time I sat down to practice, I did so with the clear intention of understanding. Soon a woman appeared, floating upon the water. Her legs were crossed in front of her, her hands upon her knees. It seemed that she too, was practicing silent time, her focus was so intense. I sat, looking, trying to see. I looked and I looked. I closed my eyes, opened them, and looked again. I asked her not to leave, to stay until I had understood. Then I continued to look. I looked until I saw it—something deep below her belly, something rotating—something black and coiled.

"Serpent," I said, "is that you?"

There was no response.

I asked to see the other women who had been appearing before me. One by one they came, each possessing the same small, coiled, black serpent.

"Serpent," I said, "wake up, serpent."

"Those who would awaken me do not remember," serpent said.

"What?" I said.

"They do not remember me," she repeated.

I paced around the interior of the cave. My head raced with thoughts and questions about what serpent had said to me earlier. I had also arrived at the time where I was to tell Lilith the final part of my last cycle of visions. This was the one that disturbed me most deeply. Part of me was glad to be finishing, yet another part met it with great resistance, not knowing what would come next.

I closed my eyes and told it to Lilith: the haunting song of the pillar, Aureillia's brutal murder and Barbara losing her serpent light, her power. . .

"Oh, my," I said, standing up suddenly. "These women, Lilith, these women who have been appearing to me, they do not remember their power. They do not remember the Goddess. The Goddess within, She too is murdered."

I walked over to the entrance of the cave and stared out at the night sky. A coldness formed inside my belly before sinking lower. "How do you live without power?" I said to the cool night air. I turned back toward Lilith. "It is worse than I thought."

"You have done well," Lilith said, with startling familiarity.

"Who are you?" I said.

She stood up and spread her wings high to the sky, her hands meeting in the air above her head so that her feathers formed a beautiful wide, arcing circle around her. "I am the Goddess," she said, looking at me.

I spread my arms wide to either side of me, then up over my head so that my hands met in the air above it. "I, too, am the Goddess," I said, returning her gaze.

# CHAPTER 28

The next morning as the sun was rising out of the sea, the voice came to me and everything became clear. All the parts of my life, everything that I had been through, all fell into place in a singular, straight line, and I understood. I understood all in a moment of crystal purity.

"Do something to help the women," the voice said. "You must do something to help these women."

But what?

I began to think about it incessantly. What could I do? I wandered the forest, down new and different trails, walked again and again the same path along the beach. I sat up with Lilith by the fire, thinking. Nothing came to me.

One night the Moon was round and huge in the sky above the cove. I left the confines of the cave and went to walk in Her full whiteness. Her reflection shone perfectly from the still waters.

I stood at the edge of the wetness watching it. If I did not know better, I might have thought there was actually a moon within the water. There it sat, within Her black depths. There even seemed to be rays shimmering up out of it toward the sky in the exact manner that they shone down from Her in the sky. It was uncanny. The same feelings were elicited from the one in the water and the one in the sky. I tried to look between them to see if there was a perceptible difference, but to my physical body there was none. Only my mind could convince me that I was not looking at two separate, yet same, Moons.

When I turned around, I was startled by the sight of Danelle standing in front of me. White light reflected off his hair, which hung in loose strands around his face, and glistened on the delicate hairs on his chest and legs. He said nothing, only stood there looking at me.

I stared back at him, trying to determine whether it was really him.

"Aureillia," he said finally. "It is not a vision. It is really me."

We moved toward each other. I could not stop looking at him, the places where his skin met the fabric of his shorts, his strong hip bones and his smell, his particular essence, reaching me, stirring up in me memory.

"Here. See," he said, placing his hands, warm and human, on my upper arms.

I placed my open palms upon his chest. It pulsed heat upon them. "Danelle," I said, remembering him. I moved my face toward him and began to trace his graceful, defined collarbone with my mouth.

He took my face into his hands. "How I've missed you," he said.

*   *   *

"How did you know I was here?" I asked him later as we sat on the beach together.

"I have known since you left," he said. "It is well known where you are."

"Why have you come only now?"

"Twenty-six moons. I was told to wait twenty-six moons," he said. "I counted each moon with a stone. I placed each stone into a circle at our meeting place until I had two circles of thirteen. Many times I did not think I could endure it."

"Twenty-six moons," I said. "Who told you that?"

"Barbara."

"Barbara!" I exclaimed, standing up.

"Yes," he said, "before she was taken back. When I went to say goodbye, she told me. She said, 'Give her time, hard as it will be for you. You must give her time. No less than twenty-six moons. When you return to her, return on the rounded moon.'"

"Oh, my," I said. I began to pace.

"Why do you act this way, Aureillia?" he asked, standing up and stopping me by placing himself in front of me.

"Oh, no," I said, moving him out of my way. "I cannot do this. I will not do this. You should not have come. Do you know what we have just done?"

I walked furiously back to the cave. "Lilith," I cried upon entering it. "Lilith, I will not do this," I screamed at her, sitting there by the fire, as calm as ever. "Make it go away. I will not."

She turned her head toward me, fire burning in her eyes. She blinked, clearing them. "Do not deny yourself the good parts of being human," she said calmly to the fire in front of her.

"Oh, no—you're not going to trick me into it, either, like before. I don't want to. I don't want to go back."

I walked up and down the cave rubbing my hands together in front of me, yanking at my own hair. I cursed the moon. I cursed Danelle. I cursed Barbara. I walked and walked until I could not walk anymore and collapsed into a pile of bones by the fire.

Lilith came to me and wrapped her feathered wings around me. "Aureillia, do not deny yourself the good parts of being human," she repeated.

I began to sob, my chest heaving against the cave floor. "Lilith, don't leave me," I said.

"It is time," she said. "It is time."

In the morning, I woke to an empty cave. A cold cave. The fire was out. I sat for a long time beside the ashes. When I finally walked to the entryway, I could see Danelle on the beach, drawing in the sand with a long stick.

I joined him. We stood together looking at the drawing. It was a circle, and within the circle were many intricate lines that almost looked like feathers. He held the stick above it, poised to destroy it.

I reached for his hand. "Please don't," I begged.

"Leave it, for just a little while."

He put the stick down. "Please come back, Aureillia," he said. "I need you."

"I will," I said, taking his hands into mine. "Not right now, but I will."

He held my hands and looked at me, and then, with the slyest look on his face, danced a quick dance with his feet, wiping away the drawing.

"Oh, no," I said, though I could not resist laughing with him. "Why must you always destroy them?"

"They are made to be destroyed," he said.

"You do it only because I ask you not to," I chided. "Perhaps. That is certainly part of it," he said, pulling me toward him onto the mixed-up dirt of the ruined drawing. "But it is only because you think you cannot create them that you like them so."

"No. No. I like them because they are beautiful, beautiful like you."

"Aureillia," he said, his face flushing slightly. He put his fingers through my hair, which had grown long.

"May I come see you again?"

"Yes. Yes, of course. I want you to," I said. "Only, the next time you come you must bring Metha with you."

# CHAPTER 29

It was Metha and Thela who were present for the bringing forth of my daughter whom I, of course, named Lilith.

Metha came bearing tonics and exercises. Exercises to open the hips, widening, widening toward eventual release.

"Aureillia," she had said when Danelle first brought her, "I am delighted. I really did not think we would ever go through this together."

She had widened with the years. This added breadth seem to accentuate her nurturing character. Her hair had stripes of white running through it, illuminating her round, black face.

"It is a very good sign when a woman of the venom conceives," she said. "It shows that the body has done well in detoxifying itself."

How was the skin able to stretch so and still remain supple? I spread the oils Metha had left me upon my expanding womb. At night I lay on the beach exposing to the moon above the moon growing within me, making a moon of my womb. Ten moons, ten cycles of sacred shedding stored within as I create other.

The feeling of the child swimming within my waters startled me at first, making real what had only seemed to be. I sat and listened to her movement—my hands following, tracing, often calming with mere presence.

As she became larger a little foot became visible, kicking me in different places depending upon where she was—once up under my breasts, once to the right side or down, onto my lower organs. A little tiny foot—kick, kick, kick—within me. The shape of a perfect little foot visible through stretching skin—small contoured ankle—I would rub with my fingers.

For a long time after I had released her I missed that foot—that kicking within. I would rub the ankle with my thumb and forefinger, close my eyes and try to remember the swimming inside me. I would say to myself, *Soon I will forget how this little foot moved within me*.

In the sands of the cove, beneath the moon, I would lie and pray for protection. For though I knew myself to be healthier than I had been in a long time, the venom, I knew, was still within me. Though Barbara had ordered Danelle to wait the twenty-six moons, she had not counted on my anger being so strong that I would neglect my-self. I had, in my time at the cove, not been taking my tonics.

Finally, I confessed to Metha the truth about my neglect.

"Only time will tell," she said, shaking her head. Then, furiously, "What could make a woman so angry that she would neglect her own body?"

I looked at her bitterly.

"I heard your prophecies," she responded. "I am aquainted with this most difficult task you were called upon to perform, but that is no excuse for rejecting the physical form, Aureillia. Prophecies or not, you are alive in this world now. How could you deny that?"

I could think of nothing to say in response.

"Now, your child will suffer due to your neglect."

"Perhaps," I said. "We shall see."

"There is no way the venom has not influenced the child which grows within you."

"Metha, must you be so hard on me? I was very upset. I was not thinking properly."

"Foolish woman! How could hurting yourself serve any pur-pose?"

"When you put it that way, it seems so clear, but at the time, I did not find a reason to care."

She clucked her tongue and sighed heavily, dropping her anger as suddenly as it had risen. "Luckily for you," she said, "you have me, and I know everything there is to know about bringing forth. And I know well about the venom," she said, lowering her voice. "It took my moth-er, but only after blinding my sister. Yes, I know well about the venom."

I looked at Metha, shocked by this unexpected information. "Metha," I asked, "Who was your mother?"

She shook her head fiercely, puffing her cheeks full of air so that they rounded her mouth into a small circle, "No," she said, closing the door to any discussion, "I will not."

As the child grew within me, it became more and more apparent that this was a child of the dolphins. All I had to do was go near the water and dolphins would appear, circling around my womb as I stood within Her. As they spoke, squeaking their high-pitched squeals, the child would remain still, listening. As they swam, she would swim within me. As I swam, they would swim around me.

Because it was a child of the dolphins, I entered the water as of-ten as I could, even bringing forth into the water.

During the time I carried her, I had many visitors. Slowly, I again became a part of the community I had left behind.

When she was still within, Danelle came asking if he had fathered the child that was growing inside me.

"I know I am required to wait until the child is released," he said, "but I simply cannot."

"Yes," I said, "it is you who fathered the child that grows within me."

What could one say to describe the smile that passed over his face at that moment, before he kissed me so strongly on the lips, I had not, for several moments, air within me.

He came to see her every day. I knew he came to see me as well, but mostly, he came to see her. I was glad for them both.

"I think you should know," I said to him one evening as we sat before the fire inside the cave, "when you came to me, that first night here at the cove, when I conceived this child, I had not been taking proper care of myself. I had not been taking the tonics to neutralize the venom within me."

"That does not surprise me," he said, "You were in a very agitated state."

"Yes, so I was. But the child, Danelle, the child that grows within me could be at risk."

"It does not feel that way to me," he said, adding a branch to the fire.

"What do you mean?"

"It does not feel to me that the child is at risk."

"How can you say that?"

"Merely a feeling. Why?" he asked, looking at me with concern. "Does it seem to you that the child is at risk?"

"No," I said slowly. "It actually does not. But, though I would like to, I cannot deny that my foolishness has endangered her."

"It could have. You are right. But I rather think it did not."

"What makes you so certain?"

"I trust Barbara."

"Barbara?"

"She would have told me more if she thought I needed to know more."

"But how could she have known?"

"She knew everything else."

"That is true," I said, stoking up the fire.

"Do not use this as another opportunity to be cruel to yourself, Aureillia."

"But Metha told me of her sister and her mother. Metha said there is no way that the child will not be influenced."

"I am familiar with Metha's story. She has suffered indeed. But that is Metha's experience. It does not have to be the same for us."

"For us?" I said, readjusting my feet below me to better handle the new weight in my belly.

"This is a risk we took together. You do not actually think you are alone in this?"

"How could you have known?" I said, leaning back, still uncomfortable. I rolled up a blanket and placed it behind my lower back.

"I did not know, but I also did not request to know. If I had taken the time to think about it, I would have known it to be a risk, but I chose not to."

"What would you have asked?"

"Whether or not you had been taking your tonics, to start."

"What would have made you ask such a thing?"

"Men too are schooled in these matters," he said. "Aureillia, because of your intense isolation in the temple during your time as a Snake priestess, there are many things which you do not know. Men too are taught to be responsible for the role we play in creating others."

"When? When is it that you are schooled in these things?"

"During initiation to male being. We are taught to be concerned about whether or not a woman is controlling her fertility—so that we know whether or not our acts are contributing to the possibility of new life. We are also taught about the dangers of conception for a Snake priestess and for the child that grows within her waters."

"But, Danelle, why is it that you never asked me?"

"Because I knew you, Aureillia."

"You knew me?"

"I saw the care you were taking of yourself and the intense care Barbara was taking of you. Perhaps I should not have assumed . . ."

"No. You were correct in your assumptions. Others you ask?"

"Always others I ask."

When the movement toward opening began and my muscles pushed toward release, Metha and Thela began busying themselves with the assisting tasks. Danelle approached Metha.

"May I stay?" he asked her.

"That is Aureillia's decision to make," she said.

"Aureillia," he said, approaching me, "may I stay?"

"Of course," I said. "Here," I offered him my arm, "help me walk down to the water."

We all went down to the cove and they took turns walking me along the shoreline or wading within Mother Sea until I felt it: an intense pain, a pain so large and enormous that it turned itself over into power. A current filled my hips and entire pelvic area with a warmth—a liquid feeling—which passed up through me and out the top of my head as her head descended through the tunnel, dark and narrow, within me.

I felt her head first emerge from between my legs and into the water as Metha eased the rest of her out.

"Metha, let me have her," I said impatiently as she stood washing her with the water.

But she would not. She kept her there, looking at her and washing her and looking at her, until hysterical sobs poured out of her. She turned her back to us and let her tears flow. She held the child to her chest, saying over and over, "She's beautiful. She's beautiful. Aureillia, you have done it again The child is well."

By the time I got my own arms around her, the child was already minutes old. She looked up at me with her little dolphin face, and I was filled with the most sudden and unexplainable love for everything and everyone, everywhere. It was an enormous feeling, extending beyond all bounds. I had never felt this large and open, this expanded. This love was free of attachment. I handed her over to Danelle and Thela, who were standing beside me in the waters, waiting. We passed the child back and forth among the four of us for so long that it became dark without our noticing.

Later, the three of them built a large fire on the beach, quite close to the water. Danelle slept in the sand beside it as Metha, Thela, and I sat close to one another in a tight circle of three. Lilith was asleep, wrapped tightly in a blanket and set in the small space between us. We all sat, heads down, looking at her.

"You are very lucky," Metha said, grasping my hand with both of hers. "This has meant so much to me."

I looked up at her. "Yes, I know," I said. "I am sorry if I have caused you more suffering. Had I known—"

"Had you known, you would not have told me, and I would not have had this opportunity to heal," Metha finished. "But let us not be deceived," she reminded. "You will continue to look for signs of the venom."

I nodded my head.

We sat quietly for a while. Only now had I time to remember the actual experience of bringing forth. "The strange thing is," I said, thinking aloud, "that when I felt myself opening for the final release of her, it was surprisingly similar to an awakening of the Serpent of Fire."

"Yes, it is true," Thela said. In Thela's face I saw the change I had only felt in my own. It was the same face and yet a different one. A face with more years, more creases, less innocence and more wisdom. The distance that had gaped between us for so long, had suddenly closed up and was gone. We had felt it the first time she had come to visit me at the cove. "It is in this way I came to know of Her. In the birth of Leida I experienced it, but the newness of the experience and my own unfamiliarity with the Serpent of Fire caused me to not pay it attention. However, after a second and third time I decided to ask around. It was after the birth of my third child that I began a serious practice toward awakening Her consciously."

"So it is that many women come to know of Her," Metha said. "Very often in bringing forth is She activated."

"Activated in bringing forth? How fascinating," I marveled. I could feel it; the beginning of something within me—a stirring, a thought, a question, an idea. "So," I mused, "one does not need to be sitting down quietly in order to awaken Her?"

"No," Thela said. The fire blazed behind her, outlining her thick curls with an orange-yellow glow. "I suppose not."

"Most definitely not," Metha said, looking still at Lilith but shaking her head from side to side. She leaned over and kissed the child lightly on the head. Metha stood up, looked at Thela and smiled, extending her hands toward her. Thela placed her hands within Metha's, who pulled her up to standing.

Together, they began to dance.

# CHAPTER 30

We stayed at the cove, my daughter and I. On warm evenings, we slept together within a blanket close to the water.

With each tug of her small, determined mouth at my nipple, I felt myself healing. Each of those tugs, strong and rhythmic, sent messages of tuggings deep within, inside me, setting healing juices flowing.

I loved the way the milk flowed out of me and into her in warm, silky streams; the way my body knew when it was time for her to eat, the sudden, surging push against the insides of my nipple right before she vocalized her hunger. I loved the liquid flow of filling her as I emptied myself.

She was thriving, there seemed to be no sign of the venom. She had the dark hair and skin of Sheena but the deep blue eyes of Danelle. It was a striking contrast, and sometimes a bit unsettling. At times she seemed a strange child indeed.

She loved to swim with the dolphins, yet many times would fight me when I tried to take her up to the above for air. She wanted to stay under for far longer than seemed safe. When I would lift her out, she would scream with such ferocity her whole body would tense up and turn red with rage. I could not understand what was happening. I could not leave her under any longer than I had. She seemed to want to never come out. I would put her back in the moment she had regained her air, but that did not satisfy her.

Only when the dolphins were in the water with us would Lilith behave in such a way. It was not the same when we swam alone—then it was just the sensuous movements of two connected bodies.

One day I was wading in the low waters, watching the dolphins: how they played together, how they touched, how they kept within each other's company, and I knew. I knew it was time for me to return. Lilith needed the company of other humans.

It was strange to return to Knossos, which was the same, save for the addition of some new buildings. Lilith was delighted by all the action, all the people in the streets, all the other children. I could hardly contain her in the front pack I carried her in. Her little head on its strong neck swung in one direction, then the other, as she tried to see and take in everything.

Entering the Center was the most eerie for me. I felt my back soften as I approached it. A flood of images and memories threatened to overtake me simply by breathing in the smells in the air surrounding it. I slowed my pace. I gently reminded myself that my duties as a Snake priestess in the temple of the Snake Goddess had been completed and I carried no further commitment there. Though I had entered through the east wing, I was sure I could smell the snakes. My stomach churned in disgust.

Danelle was surprised to see me enter the workshop. He dropped his tools and almost knocked his stool over as he stood to approach us. "You've come back! You've come back. Oh, thank you," he said as his arms encompassed us.

I looked up into his face. Bright red lines ran through the whites of his eyes. "Your eyes, Danelle, your eyes. You must take more care."

"Yes," he said, taking Lilith from the pack to himself. He hugged her close to his chest, then nuzzled his face into her belly. She squealed with delight.

I looked around his workshop. He had moved his work table into the middle of it. There it sat, a cluttered mess in the middle of the clear-topped student tables. The light from the window shone directly down onto it. Something shimmered. I walked over to it. The shimmering object was underneath one of the enlarging glasses. Smaller sparkles spread around it. I looked through the glass. It was a gold ring, the glitterings around it were the fragments of gold that had been carved off.

Onto the small oval surface of the ring he was involved in carving an entire scene. I leaned in closer toward the glass. *No wonder your eyes are red*, I thought to myself when I comprehended the minuteness of the work. On this tiny surface there were priestesses in ritual attire, an olive tree, the sacred labrys, the sun and crescent moon, and a bee. "May I pick it up to see it better?" I asked.

"Yes, of course."

I brought the ring close to my eyes and studied it further, becoming aware of masks with stinger-like projections on the priestesses. "The festival of the bees," I said. "Danelle, this is incredible. Who is it for? Gold? I have never known you to work in gold."

"There are more," he said. "There's a whole cycle of them. I'm doing them for the women."

"Women? What women?"

"Your women. The women you told me about, the ones who appeared to you at the cove."

"What? You?"

"Yes. After you told me about them, I could not get them out of my mind. I felt I too needed to do something."

"Here," he said, getting down a small box, "here are two more, already finished."

I took them, one at a time, first looking at them close to my eyes, then placing them under the glass. One had priestesses in ecstatic dance, arms held out and up in sacred gesture toward the presence of the Goddess. Divine energy flowed around them in the form of many small dots.

The other one had women and men in ritual attire, dancing in celebration of first fruits. The design had a large tree running through it, its trunk and branches separating it into the four quarters of the moon and the annum. There were so many small figures within each quarter of this ring it was diffiult to conceive how he had ever managed it. Clearly from the state of his eyes, it had been a less than easy accomplishment.

I was moving between the enlarging glasses, observing one, then another. I could not stop looking at them. "This is some of the best work you have ever done," I said.

"I intend to bury them somewhere. Somewhere I know no one will find them for a very long time. For this reason I chose gold, as it is known to be the longest lasting."

"Why rings?" I asked, pulling one over my finger—for which it was far too large.

"From what I know of people in the surrounding lands, rings are used to indicate importance. I thought that by carving them onto the surface of rings, whoever it is that discovers them might be more inclined to pay them attention. Of course, I am using the largest size available to give myself more surface area. It is rather challenging to try to fit an entire belief system on the surface of a few rings. I am not at all sure that I am succeeding."

"Hmm," I said, looking at them again. "True, it is difficult to know what the person who uncovers them will make of them. At the very least, the artistic accomplishment of them would give anyone cause to ponder over the identity of their creator."

"Such flattery," he said, smiling with so much humility that my heart expanded. He held the ring up to Lilith, whose eyes crossed in trying to focus on it.

"Too small for you," he said, waving his hand in front of her eyes to help them refocus.

"I know I did not ask you about it," he continued. "I wanted to surprise you, but then it turned into a larger project than I had expected. I hope you do not mind."

"No. No, of course I do not mind. I am surprised and I must say, once again, intensely jealous."

"Jealous?"

"Yes, jealous. I have not even figured out what it is I shall do, and here you are already doing it—and something so wonderful," I said, pointing toward his worktable.

"Well, Aureillia, you know what that means. You will know soon and it will be much better."

I laughed at this but became serious when I noticed again his eyes. "But your eyes," I said, touching my fingers to the deep creases on either side of them. "You must be more concerned over your eyes."

"Yes, well," he said to Lilith, "perhaps now I will be."

Lilith and I moved into an open room in Thela's block. The people of Knossos seemed to have mixed feelings about my return. Many looked rather fearful and would back away from me or cross to the opposite side of the walkway when they noticed me approaching them. Though it made my insides flinch with pain, I was not surprised. I had prepared myself well for just this reaction during my many moons of isolation at the cove.

This being the case, the opposite reaction surprised and stirred my insides with warmth and gratitude. So it was with the women of Thela's block who welcomed me, accepting Lilith and me among them with the greatest generosity. I understood this to be only an extension of their feelings toward Thela, and considered myself very lucky.

Sitting around the fire in the central court with the women of Thela's block in the evenings was a delight I had never expected to share again.

It had been so long since I had slept in a bed and cooked and eaten among others, since I had awakened in the morning to the sounds of human voices and children playing. It had been so long since I had shared varied conversation and daily discourse. For me, all this was strange at first, but Lilith was overjoyed with the presence of so many others. The children of the block included her instantly, and Thela's daughters, of which there were now three, could not get enough of her.

A soon as Lilith began to walk, she was taken with the block's children on their daily adventures. It was difficult for me, at first, to let her go. This separation from her was so intense and tugging, since I'd had her to myself for so long. For a while I cringed over the resentment I felt toward others' demands and expectations that I share her. Recognizing these feelings made me even more glad that I had returned when I had. I had clearly developed an unhealthy dependence on her.

Seeing Lilith interact with other people, especially other children, loosened this holding inside me. It reminded me of my own youth and how much my friends had meant to me. I would not have wanted anyone to keep that from me.

Our relationship changed and grew into this new, healthier space. From her I sensed relief in the realization that there was more than one person for her to lean on, to need, to care for her, to hope and expect from. I saw her small being stretching and expanding in the possibility of more people to love and be loved by, opening to it willingly.

So much the company of women had to offer me. Together we raised the children, sharing all the duties, alternating nights of obligation with nights of release. Lilith had been tossed into the pool of children and I into the group of nurturing adults.

Leida, Thela's first daughter, seemed uncomfortable around me still. I resolved to change this between us. I began to make it a point to not let her discomfort keep me away. Knowing that the only way she would get over her discomfort would be for her to get to know me, I made sure to speak to her every day about even the smallest things. She was a small-framed girl, close to the age of initiation. In fact, it seemed she would be arriving at initiation later than most. In so many ways she looked like Thela, but her face had a broadness and a width about it that Thela's pointed one had not. Her forehead was wide and strong. Her hair was long, wavy and deep, deep black. One day I asked her to accompany me on a walk.

"I suppose it is difficult for you," I said, deciding to broach the subject, "for you remember. To a child I am sure I must have been quite a frightening aunt and I am sorry for that, for you seem to be frightened still."

"Yes, I was," she responded, "but as for now, I am no longer frightened. I am in awe of you."

I stopped walking and looked at her in surprise. It was not a response I had expected.

"I feel you have been so brave and so strong," she said. Beads of sweat had formed above her lips. "Oh, Aunt Aureillia, you are the most wonderful woman I have ever known, and I find myself feeling unworthy of you."

"Unworthy?" I said. "Leida, how you catch me off guard. These feelings were not the ones I had expected to encounter. "Please do not mistake my previous distraction as means to wonder why I neglected my duty as an aunt. I regret the time I lost with you. Every inch of you is worthy of me or anyone."

She smiled and breathed in deeply. A great sigh of relief passed between us both, but there was something, still I felt it. We walked on. It was an intensely hot day and I was looking forward to reaching the water so that I could cool myself within it.

"Tell me about the snakes," Leida said. "What was it like, with the snakes?"

I looked at her but she did not look at me, a deliberate avoidance of eye contact. I had never talked about the snakes to anyone outside the temple. I was not sure I could or should. Also, no one had ever asked. "Why do you wish to know?"

"They terrify me so," she said.

"Why would you fear them? You have no relationship with them," I said, then teased, "do you?"

"I am not sure," she said, looking at the ground.

"Leida," I said, stopping her with my hands and turning her toward me, my insides shaking with fear, "Leida, is there something you are not telling me?"

She continued to look down, tears running from her eyes. I lifted her face to look at me.

"Sometimes," she struggled, "sometimes, I think I hear things."

I held my tongue, not wanting to upset the poor girl further. "Have you told your mother of this?"

"I dare not."

"Leida, more than hear things, the question is, do you know things?"

"Yes," she admitted. "Yes, I do. It scares me so." I put my arms around her. I held her shaking body within them. I rocked her and myself together and I began to weep silent tears. *So it goes. So it continues*, I thought to myself. *Oh, Thela. Thela. Thela.*

"Thela," I said to Leida's mother the next morning upon our meeting in the central court, "join me for a walk? To the Cave of Medena?"

"Medena?" she repeated, surprised. "Yes."

In our dresses with large pockets we set out together, as we had so many times before. When we reached Dolphin Cove I stopped. I sat down and patted the sand beside me for her to join me. "Thela" I said, when she had settled herself, "do you remember the day so long ago when I became aware of my gift?"

"Oh, yes—I shall never forget it. It was right here, in this very place."

"Yes, it was," I said, "I will never forget what you did for me that day, how you stayed beside me, asking nothing but offering all."

"We went to Medena."

"My first time."

"Oh, to youth," she smiled.

I closed my eyes. My stomach turned and churned. "Thela, there is someone, someone who had just such a discovery, someone who let it go unnoticed, someone who needs you to give to her what you gave to me."

"Leida?" she said. "Are you speaking of Leida?" Her face was filled with red passion and fury. "Why did she not tell me herself?"

"Because of me," I said. "Because of me she is unable to be proud and excited."

"I do not wish it for her, Aureillia," she cried, standing and stepping back from me. "I do not wish it for her. I will not, cannot go through it again." Thela stopped, put her hands in front of herself, and made a pushing motion with them toward me. She turned and faced the water.

I sat and watched the wind blow at her, how it first lifted her dress and hair before whipping it back.

"I suspected," she said when I approached her. "No. I knew. Aureillia, I have been selfish. I am so ashamed," she confessed. "I know exactly when and where it happened; I pretended not to notice. I hoped if I ignored it she would forget and it would just go away." She covered her mouth with her hands. "How terribly unfair I have been, asking her not to become what she is because of my own pain."

"Oh, Thela," I said, "how on earth are we going to do this?"

We took turns following each other to the Cave of Medena, Mother of Darkness.

If I thought the path was difficult the first time, as a girl, it was extremely challenging as a woman. Our sadness dispersed into laughter, watching each other fall face first into the water, grasping desperately at each other's extended hands, crawling clumsily up giant rocks and boulders, drenching wet.

"Whose idea was this?" we kept asking each other before breaking into hysterical laughter.

"It was yours the first time," I would say.

"Yes, and yours this time," she would counter, then it would start again, the laughter; the deep and hearty, the echoing and joyous, the shared and united, comedy.

Finally we reached the cave.

Her sudden, dark silence fell upon us, forcing us into our thinking selves. When we entered the shrine, we each placed an offering for Leida and for our own torn and tattered souls—not to mention our clothing—and I turned to Thela. "Sing," I said. "Oh, sing for me, please?"

# CHAPTER 31

I knew now the time had come. I knew for Leida's sake I had to make peace with the snakes. If I did not, I could be of no assistance to her and I could indirectly and unknowingly bring harm to her. But I resisted. I fought.

I entered the temple. Alone, I approached the pit. I dared not look upon the sacred sculpture for all the rage and resentment that had grown in me. I sat only by the pit, looking upon the snakes, trying to let myself feel it, but I could not. I fled the temple remaining unquiet for days.

The one thing Lilith missed since our return to Knossos was the dolphins. I began taking her to Dolphin Cove in the mornings to swim with them. It seemed she needed them to survive. When I could not take her, Danelle did.

Something strange but intriguing happened to her when she swam with them. It was as though the life-force returned to her. She became relaxed and regained her color. Her eyes recovered their deep spark.

At the same time, she terrified me, staying again under the water for periods of time that seemed beyond safe. I feared for her. I would go down and, almost feeling as though I was interrupting something, call her up to surface. Though she had not yet many words, when she came above, she would say things like, "No, Mama. Stay longer," or, "Leave Lilith alone". Sometimes she would scream at me violently. It became a daily struggle, one that I was losing. It was exhausting. I began to dread going.

One morning as we swam, I heard murmurings from within the water, as though overhearing a distant conversation. I lifted my head out of the water and explored the surrounding waters and beach. There were no other people present. I submerged my head and again I heard it. I lifted my head out of the water again to silence. I shook my head and submerged myself again. It seemed like the sound of many people talking at once. I tried to listen. A dolphin swam close to me and as she did, one singular voice became louder. *It cannot be,* I thought to myself, but as she swam closer again, the voice grew louder and clearer.

"Are you talking to me?" I asked her with the voice inside my own head.

"We talk to those who are willing to listen," the dolphin answered.

My heart pumped so loudly within me that it overpowered their voices. I swam to shore to catch my breath. *It must be the venom*, I thought. *It has given me the ability to transmute the language of the dolphins.*

Lilith had followed me to shore, tugging and pulling at my arm. "Back, Mama. Back, Mama," she implored. Then she put her little face close to mine. "Happy, Mama?" she asked, tilting her head to one side, eyebrows raised. "Happy?"

"Oh," I said pulling her to me and hugging her for her sweetness, but she tugged away and looked out toward the water, toward the dolphins, longingly.

"Oh, no, Lilith," I said, too loudly, quite scaring her so that she burst into tears from the strong, sudden outburst.

"Is this what is happening to you?" I said. "Can you hear them? Can you hear the dolphins?"

She nodded her head eagerly, pulling me toward the water again. "Dolphins talk Lilith," she said. "Yes. Yes. Back, Mama?"

So now I knew. The venom was running through Lilith. I had poisoned my daughter.

I wandered. I lay awake at night. I worried incessantly. I sat beside her as she slept, asking for forgiveness. I knelt beside her bed. I rocked upon my knees. I stroked and stroked her head.

Together we returned to the dolphins. Together we listened. These dolphins—they had so much to say. It was no wonder that Lilith was captivated by them; no wonder she became angry when I pulled her into the above, interrupting a story.

Floating side by side in the water, we listened together, coming up for breath at the same time. And yes, it did seem I was able to stay under longer than before; the distraction of the stories somehow lengthening the breath held within.

I tried to have the dolphins join us on shore, in lower waters, so that we did not have to be concerned about taking breaks for air. But, unless I was fully submerged, I could not understand them. It seemed water was the conductor of the sound; the water and the transmuted venom within us a necessary combination.

The dolphins told us many stories of the many different things they had seen within the waters and their encounters with beings who made their homes on the edges of the lands since the Goddess had filled the seas. They talked of a time when the earth was new, when the air was colder, when the lands were in different places. Their stories were vast and varied, but the most captivating thing about them, the thing that made one want to hear more and more, was the sheer pleasure they took in telling them.

We would listen for a time, then bid them farewell. I would be left thinking about what they had said, but for Lilith, this did not seem to be the case.

She needed it and fared better in the days that we swam with the dolphins, but it was not something she continued to think about after it had ended. It was something she experienced fully as it was happening. The experience nourished her and filled her. Like morning meal, it was a necessary requirement for the day, but not something she was left ruminating over.

It was a relief to have the daily morning struggles at the beach, for the moment, gone. Though I continued to worry over her desperately, I felt I was understanding better this strange child. In her too, there seemed to be a great sense of relief.

After a while of early morning listening, the dolphins began to engage in long silences between stories. During this silence, they and Lilith would turn their attention to me. The silences made me uncomfortable; it was clear I was missing something. But what?

One day in one of these silences, I said, "Where did you get all of these stories? In what manner were they communicated to you?"

They did not respond; they only looked from one to another and remained silent. "And what, I wonder, would you have to say about Minoa?" Again, all simply looked at me, keeping silent.

Lilith and I climbed the narrow, overgrown path behind the cove that led back toward Knossos. Halfway up the path, I stopped. "That's it!" I said. "Lilith, quickly—we must go back to the water." We ran back to the water and called the dolphins near.

"I was wondering," I said, "would you let me tell you the story of Minoa that you may include it in your stories, that people in the future might remember us?"

"We thought you'd never ask," the dolphins said, giggling amongst themselves. Lilith giggled with them. She clapped her hands. She looked at me, beaming with pride.

It was fun preparing this story. After being tied down to the prophecy form for so long, to be able to expand, to take time, to use length. It was hard to decide what to include and what to leave out. It needed, above all, to be a good story. I worked on it for a long time in my head, jotting down notes for myself, then I taught it to the dolphins. I told them over and over, and they repeated it back to me until I liked the way it sounded. When I liked the way it sounded, it was complete.

It is this which I did for the women.

Danelle had completed his series of gold rings. When I had completed my "Ode to Minoa" we began to spend days walking the island together, looking for the perfect place to bury the rings. It was a wonderful thing to do, walking together, side by side, exploring new paths and discovering places we had never known before.

But the rings—where to bury the rings? We had walked and walked and still no place seemed right.

"I did not expect it to be so difficult," Danelle said one day, sounding quite discouraged. We were resting, sitting next to each other on separate rocks on a hilly, wooded pathway.

I did not respond. "What is it, Aureillia?" he asked. "You seem so troubled."

"Indeed, I am sore to the bone over what I have done to my daughter. There seems to be no distraction large enough to remove my thoughts from it. I do not know that I can bear it."

"Are you speaking of the venom?"

I nodded my head.

"Aureillia, I cannot understand. Why is it that you choose to see this as something bad?"

"I have transmitted poison to her, Danelle. How can that be good?"

"You have passed her the gift of being able to understand the language of the dolphins. What an amazing way for a child to experience the world! Why can you not see that? You have passed her the wisdom of the serpent without having to suffer the pain of the bite."

"But the venom, the venom could harm her physically."

"Yes, this part is true, but is also done, over. Now you know. The question is what to do? That is the issue here, not how horrible you are."

I looked at him, feeling rather wounded. "Danelle, I have never known you to be so harsh."

"I have never known you to be so foolish," he retorted, standing up. "I find myself rather disappointed."

"But of course I would feel badly. How could I not feel badly?"

"It is not that you feel badly that disappoints; it is the persistent ill thoughts directed toward yourself. What could cause such a change?"

"A change?"

"If there is a problem, one searches for solutions, one seeks, one moves forward. You used to do this. But now, now you seem stuck, stuck on something that serves no purpose."

I said nothing, only picked up a stick and thrust it repeatedly into the earth beside me. Flecks of dirt and rocks flew up around it. I continued, beginning to hollow out a hole.

"I have been thinking," Danelle said, his tone calmer, "perhaps there is a series of tonics we could start her on. Would it be all right with you if I discussed this with a temple healer?"

I stopped digging. I looked at him. I felt resentment. Why was I so muddled up and he so clear headed? "Danelle, why have I not thought of this myself?"

"You are spending all your time worrying. You seem unable to see anything else."

"No," I said quickly. "You are correct about everything except that. It is not the worrying that blinds me. I dare say it is something other."

"What is it?"

"It is anger, Danelle. It burns at me."

"Anger? Anger at whom?"

"At the snakes and what they told me. Anger at the things I have seen, the things I have been made to witness."

"It is not the fault of the snakes."

"Then whose fault is it?" I said. I was pointing the stick at him as he stood above me. "Who can I be angry at? You tell me," I said. "Tell me who to be angry at?"

"Not at me," he said, grabbing the stick out of my hand and flinging it through the air so that it hit the branches of a nearby tree.

"Forgive me, Aureillia," he said, sitting again beside me. "I do not know the answer. It is a very difficult question. There really is no one to be angry at except maybe She who chose you to to this, and that is distressing indeed."

"Yes, yes—I know. It is Her I am angry with because I cannot find a use for the information." I was missing my stick. I began to bang my fists into my own thighs. "Barbara told me, she told me not to do this. She told me I would find goodness in what I have done, but I cannot. I cannot see any purpose it serves, and then, this anger—it seems to only fuel the anger. This intense rage. It fills me up. I fear it shall overcome me."

"Yes," Danelle said, nodding his head, looking at me with great concern. "It is clear that you suffer from it. You must find a way to release it."

"Release it?" I said, looking at him. The wind blew lightly at his hair. I felt it blow at mine. "Release it," I repeated.

# CHAPTER 32

I was stunned when the recruiter from the temple of the Butterfly came to me, requesting my presence as a priestess.

I had been in the kitchen washing up the pots and bowls from morning meal. When I saw her enter the block, I remembered that I had never returned to them as I had promised I would to discuss the details of my last vision. I thought this was why she had come. I approached her apologetically. I had left so many things undone when I had fled. It was taking me some time to remember them all.

As I drew near her, she stood still and held the labryses that she carried in either hand up and out in front of her. I stopped suddenly, recognizing the gesture of sacred ritual.

"The Butterfly Goddess desires you as one of her priestesses," she sang, bringing the labryses to rest in the air over each of my shoulders.

"Me?" I said, placing my hands upon my chest in shock. "Why would she want a used-up Snake priestess?"

"You have wandered the darkness and come to the light. You are woman reborn. Your wisdom would be useful to many." I stood there in the courtyard of my new block with this woman, much younger than I, remembering the time, years before, when Barbara—then much older than I—had come to me in a similar way. I thought of my initiation into female being, how I had wished to become something other than a Snake priestess, and I felt it within me—two ends of a circle meeting.

"I do not wish to be a butterfly," I said, at once surprising and affirming. "I wish to be a woman of the feathers. I wish to be a bird. Do you have room for a bird among the butterflies?"

The recruiter's face became puzzled, her eyes distanced themselves. "I will have to speak to my leader of this," she said.

"Oh, yes. Yes, you should," I said. "I await your answer."

She turned and walked away, tripping over her feet, which seemed to have become suddenly large and cumbersome.

* * *

Word spread quickly through Knossos about what had transpired between the temple recruiter and me. The town was aflutter with it.

Danelle and I sat by the fire in the court of his block. Lilith was asleep in her bed in his room.

"I know why you want to be a bird," he whispered into my ear.

"Do you?" I answered, thinking he was being playful.

"How is it that you know?"

"I saw Her," he said. "I shall never forget it. She is the most powerful thing I have ever seen."

"You saw Her? When?"

"That first night that I came to you at the cove. I was very upset after you walked away from me. I tried to follow after you but could not determine where you had gone. I tried to rest but was unable to. When the sun began to rise, filling the air around me with sudden light, I saw the opening of the cave. I was about to walk to it when She appeared, a dark presence in the entryway. I stood there, below, not sure of what I was seeing until She spread Her wings, until She began to flap them, until they took Her to flight."

"Danelle," I whispered, looking into his face, "I did not think I would ever be able to share Her with anyone."

"You must share Her with me," he whispered back. "I want all of you. Don't you know that by now?" He looked at me, his eyes never wavering from mine. "Here," he said, pressing something into my hand, "I made you something."

I closed my fingers around it. A round stone. I could feel the lines carved into it.

"I am afraid to look at it," I said.

"Why?"

"I am not sure I want to know what it is going to tell me."

"But you must," he said, "or you would not have told me."

I lifted my hand to my chest and opened my fingers slowly. I gasped at the sight I beheld on the stone before me. There, carved into thick, black marble was the image of a woman with wide and spreading, large and encompassing, feathered wings. She wore the tiered skirt and exposed breasts of a priestess. A narrow, beaked head. Her feet were engaged in rapid movement: ecstatic dance.

There were no words—only the repetitive movement of my fingers traveling over and over again the work of his hands, tracing again and again the flowing rhythm, the beauty, the movement he had captured. The marble was cool and smooth and thick with power. I brought it to my lips. I closed my eyes and pressed it against them.

"I am not sure that I am strong enough," I said.

"I know that you are," he said.

He put his hand into his pocket and pulled out a thin, sturdy rope. He took the seal stone from me and began to lace the rope through a small hole that was already drilled into it. In the darkness, I had not been able to see it.

"You drilled a hole into it?"

"Better mine than the sloppy one you would have had someone else put through it," he said, holding the two ends up close to his face and knotting them together.

"I thought you did not want them to be worn around the neck. I would have tried to respect that, I think."

"There are some things you simply need to surrender to," he said. He put the rope over my head and around my neck so that the seal stone hung down onto my chest. "Yes," he said, observing me wearing it. "Yes. It becomes you."

The next day Helena, the leader of the temple of the Butterfly, came to me. She wore a purple dress, which hung loosely around her with long flowing sleeves.

"We welcome you in any way you wish to serve," she said, placing her hands, brown and strong, upon mine. "We are all daughters of the same Mother."

I bowed to her in sacred gesture. "Thank you," I said.

"Come to the temple when you are ready. We shall work together."

I returned to my room and climbed up on a chair so that I could reach the bag I had put up high, on the tallest shelf. In it were feathers that She, Lilith of the Cave, had shed and that I had collected. I sat down. I began to sew myself wings.

I returned again to the snakes. Again I sat over the pit. Though the smell was repulsive, I forced myself to receive it, taking it in more deeply with every lengthening breath, allowing it to enter me and fill me until I was willing to accept it. The longer I stared into the pit, the longer I forced myself to breath, the clearer it became.

That, down there, writhing within—that which I was choosing to reject—was a part of me, the biggest part. *The snakes have given me much*, I thought. *Indeed, the snakes have made me who I am.*

I could never leave them behind.

But if I could not leave them behind, how could I take them with me?

I had observed something during my time in the water with the child Lilith. I had noticed how, when I told the dolphins my story, she did not understand. She watched me with a confused expression. It was only when they sang it back to me that she turned to me, smiling in comprehension.

She could not make use of the information until the dolphins had transmuted it. This I needed to do with the snakes.

I stared into the pit, letting my eyes go. The snakes moved themselves around the interior of the pit, forming first a spiral, then a spiral within a spiral, then an intricate pattern within that.

"Oh, my," I said.

I walked quickly out of the temple and up the steps to the temple of the Butterfly. "Helena," I said, almost too loudly, when I found her. "Please, I need to enter again the labyrinth."

* * *

The darkness, the complete and engulfing silence, is shocking, as shocking as the first time.

Inside this darkness, I feel along. It is much different than I remember it. I am much taller—all around bigger—and this time, I know where I am.

I make use of some of the tricks I learned before, quickly getting down on my hands and knees. Being larger, there is need for me to lie down and slither sooner. This time, I reflect back on last time, feeling the changes within myself—the events and passage of time wedged between, enclosed and within, these two separate trips.

I crawl along, surprised by how much I have brought into the labyrinth with me, dismayed when it is thoughts of Barbara that overtake me. Images of her enter my mind and I push them away.

I have not come here to mourn.

To the pain which threatens to well up within me, I say, "no".

I have come here for other purposes.

They persist, as do I. My trip through the labyrinth becomes a battle: me pushing and pulling at the thoughts within my own mind. Though I think I remember all the tricks, though I thought I knew the way, my distraction leads me into a place I have not encountered before.

I am squeezed into the tightest space. The ceiling is low above me, the walls are close around me. I fear I shall not get out before I have no breath. I wonder if I would be better off sliding backward, but decide to continue to tunnel and burrow slowly forward. It is very difficult for I cannot lift any part of my body to help in the forward movement. I must push along ever so slowly in a slither—the movement needing to come from my hips. I can feel the places where the bones rub against the stone, the skin becoming scraped and bruised. I cannot lift my head and, though I know this, I continue to instinctively lift it, each time banging the back of it on the wall of rock above me. "Ouch," I scream out of frustration, only to hit it again when I scream. My mouth is dry and full of dust. My lungs ache in want of air and there is Barbara. There she sits, on the edge of my bed in my room beneath the temple of the Snake Goddess. It is the day of my initiation into full priestess. She is handing them to me, pushing them toward me with urgency—the two feathers of a snake eagle. "Swallow Her, Aureillia," she is saying, her eyes sparkling with intensity. "Swallow Her whole."

"Eagle?" I say. "I thought myself to become an owl."

"Only eagle can swallow snake whole."

When I exited the labyrinth, there was a crowd of people there to greet me. I was startled to see so many residents of Knossos welcoming me back; accepting me in my new role. I walked toward Helena, who stood in front of the crowd holding my wings. When I reached her, she placed them over my shoulders. "Priestess of the bird, you now become," she said.

The crowd cheered. They clapped their hands.

I looked at them. I smiled. My whole being filled with gratitude. I bowed toward them in sacred gesture. Sunlight reflected off the seal stone upon my chest. I looked at it, noticing, for the first time, the long, narrow head of an eagle.

"Helena," I said, as we walked in procession toward the west court, where there was to be a reception, "I had thought myself to become an owl, but it appears I am to be an eagle—a snake eagle."

"A snake eagle?" she said. "How interesting. This makes snake your prey, your food, a source of nourishment." She looked at me. "Indeed, digestion is needed," she said, nodding her head. "Assimilation."

"Assimilation?" I echoed. "Assimilation," I repeated, feeling the line of people growing longer behind me.

"My wings," I said, stopping and turning toward her. "My wings are incomplete."

# CHAPTER 33

"I found the perfect place," Danelle said, "you must come, now."

I followed behind him, wondering what we were doing. It soon became clear to me that he was leading me to our meeting place on the hill overlooking the sea.

"We have been looking much too hard in all the wrong places," he said when we arrived there. "I can think of no better place to leave the ring seals than right here."

I looked around at the sea stretched out in front of us, the hill sloping in toward it, the sky beyond. I felt the sense of something—that something magical about this place that we had always felt—and the possibility of others in the future feeling it as well. "Yes. You are right. It is perfect," I said. "When?"

"Tomorrow. At sunrise."

"Just you and I?"

"Just you and I."

The next morning we met at Danelle's workshop. He placed all five of the ring seals inside a small clay jar and closed it tight, then put the jar in his pocket. Together, each carrying a shovel, we ascended the hill. Underneath the fig tree that had offered us so much shade and shelter, we dug a deep hole. Into the hole we placed the jar. Then, each taking turns, one shovelful of dirt at a time, we covered it back up until it reached the level of the ground again. We flattened and flattened the space of the opening with our patting hands until there was no indication that the earth had ever moved there. We kneeled on either side of it.

"I wonder," Danelle said, looking down at the spot. "I wonder who will find them and when. I wish I could have some way of knowing."

But I was looking at him. "Danelle, thank you," I said.

He smiled. He took my hands into his. Together they were clasped over the covered opening.

"Will we meet again?"

"Many times."

"Will we remember each other?"

"Always."

* * *

The dance of release must be practiced outside on a tall hill with an open view of the world around it. It must be practiced often and with clear intention.

Rory and Zula returned to help me. They taught me the form. They watched me perform it. When I thought there was nothing left to let go of, they encouraged me to let go even further, pointing out to me the places within me where I had allowed it to become me, where I had attached to it.

They taught me well, that I may teach others.

They told me, "When you dance the dance of release, remember us. Remember the strong women to the south. Remember early women who gave birth to us all, who—when there was little food to be had—kept us alive with their moist, nurturing bodies; who learned to farm and to keep animals, who learned to build and create, but most of all who learned to dance and in their dancing learned to love the Goddess through their bodies."

And yes, Barbara had thought of everything, for when I finished sewing the two snake eagle feathers to either side of my wings, I knew the time had come. I was ready.

In a small ball upon the earth, I begin, my feathered wings wrapped around me. I slowly rise, spine unfolding as my feet begin to move up and down. Up and down they move, down and up upon the earth, upon this clay—pounded firm from so much dancing—until they pulse fire, becoming claws.

The power, rising up through me, straightens my body, lifting breasts high (opening) as wings begin to extend (extending out and up) up and down, down and up—flapping (loosening, freeing) flapping, until it has all left me, until I have let it all go and I feel Her (I feel Her entering me) Her fiery breath pulsing, once again, claiming Her proper place within me.